MIGRAT. . . .

MILOŠ TSERNIANSKI was born in 1893, the son of a
modest notary. He early discovered in himself a vocation as
a writer, nourished by reading French, German, Hungarian
and Russian authors. In August 1914 he was arrested,
recruited into the Austrian army – and sent to fight his
fellow-Serbs. After the war he settled in Belgrade, wrote
stories, plays, poetry, contributed articles to the press,
taught history in a school. In 1929 he wrote *Migrations* in
the version here published; twenty years later he was to
take it up again and continue it with a further volume. After
a spell in Berlin as press attaché at the Jugoslav embassy, he
joined the embassy staff in Rome in 1939. In 1940, with the
Axis invasion of Jugoslavia, he escaped to London, where he
was to live for many years in exile, scraping a living as a hotel
porter, while his wife made rag dolls. Not until 1956 was he
"discovered" in his native land, where his works began to be
collected and published. In 1965 he returned to Belgrade,
to a hero's welcome in literary circles. Here he wrote a
record of emigrants' lives, which was also a recollection of
his twenty-five English years. He died in Belgrade in 1977.
With Ivo Andrić, the Nobel laureate, Tsernianski is now
considered the greatest poet and novelist Serbia has pro-
duced in modern times.

Miloš Tsernianski

MIGRATIONS

Volume I

Translated from the Serbo-Croatian
by Michael Henry Heim

HARVILL
An Imprint of HarperCollinsPublishers

First published in Serbo-Croatian with the title
Seobe
by Nolit, Belgrade, 1978
First published in Great Britain in 1994
by Harvill
an imprint of HarperCollinsPublishers,
77–85 Fulham Palace Road,
Hammersmith, London W6 8JB

1 3 5 7 9 8 6 4 2

A CIP catalogue record for this book
is available from the British Library.

This translation was made possible in part through
a grant from the Wheatland Foundation, New York.

ISBN 0 00 271512 0 hardback
0 00 273004 9 paperback

Set in New Caledonia
by Servis Filmsetting Ltd
Printed and bound in Great Britain by
Redwood Books, Trowbridge, Wiltshire

1

An Endless Blue Circle.
In It a Star

For a day now willows had been rising out of the mist and clouds tumbling lower and lower. The hollow where the river ran was murky, impassable, the land black, invisible, rain-soaked.

The marshland hummed and buzzed out in the darkness. The glow of moonlight emerged from the swamp, then vanished in the night, which came and went, wringing wet, came and went, never-ending, dampening the sleeper's massive chest and belly, hot and bloated, girthed in ramskin, fleece drenched with sweat. Water seeping drop by drop through rushes, and through the dense darkness a frog jumping closer and closer.

Intermittent barking, intermittent crowing, from midnight on, but in the distance; the dull thud of hooves a constant presence, nearby beneath the snow, as if from underground. Frequent stirrings seized him, then passed, like a rocking in the darkness that creeps beneath shoulders and between ribs as they shiver from the cold. He could not distinguish the darkness around him from the darkness within him, and staring wide-eyed into the gloom he saw nothing. True, he heard the jumping frog at his head, but immediately thereafter he was overcome with sleep, and everything sank back into the heavy odour of ramskin on which the upper part of his body lay next to his wife's head.

1

Kicked by a horse in the knee several days before, while gathering his regiment, he still woke in the night in pain, but he was so tired that the pain soon passed, as did a great lethargy and lassitude in the bones. Thus he woke every hour, moaned, gnashed his teeth, and immediately fell asleep again.

Yet the things he saw in those fleeting moments of half-sleep: the river beneath the sloping banks filling the night with its flow; moonlight on the rushing water, in the fissures and gorges; reeds along the windows and on the roofs dripping their countless drops; clouds settling lower and lower; count-less luxuriant willows.

Rocking again in sleep, he spun, ablaze in a riot of colours, between unbounded heights and unlimited depths until the rain trickling through the thatch woke him once more. Only then did his turbid consciousness register the barking and crowing. He opened his eyes in the darkness and saw nothing. Though he thought he saw, far above, an endless blue circle. In it a star.

Suddenly the rocking ceased and the humming in his head broke off; he knew he was awake. He lay there in the dark with his eyes wide open, stunned, shivering with cold, dreaming no longer. He heard the barking and crowing; he heard his wife, who had fallen asleep on his arm, breathing against his chest; so still was the hut, he even heard the sound of his neck stretching. But through a crack in the boards he saw a stream of light, and was completely awake. It was time to go.

The light came from a fire laid the night before by his men, who had spread out – some by themselves, others with their wives and children – under the eaves of a sty near the meadow where the stables were. His first clear thought of the day was a battle cry imagined rather than heard: he thought he saw his men running towards him, one after the other, in terrifying charge formation, fully armed, long rifles in their hands and khanjars in their teeth, as if taking part in a drill; he saw every man's face, recognized them all, recalled where each had lain.

Thus did everything outside, in the dark rain, pass before his wide-open eyes: the slope and the Danube below, the barges that would take the men upstream, the countless willows, the bogs, the blue fallow, the red bushes.

Suddenly the sweep on the well creaked, there was a knock on the door, and when he gave a start, it was as if everything in the dark, unseen and unheard till then, had come alive with him, and he heard the pounding of hooves and the raucous barking of dogs nearby. A large flock of crows must have flown past as well, because the night and the sky were filled with cawing.

And while, still in the dark, sweaty and naked, for he always slept naked, he worked to disentangle himself from the bedding, extricate himself from the ramskin, she awoke and, all but wild with fear, felt her way to the hearth, blew on the ashes, and uncovered a few embers. She lit a candle, which illuminated her, all of her, and threw an enormous shadow of him on the wall. She let out a scream and began to wail, to hug him and cover his chest, shoulders, neck, and ears with kisses.

It was nearly two weeks since the Marquis Ascanio Guadagni, commander of the town of Osijek, had ordered him to equip three hundred crack soldiers to march against France, and she had not ceased her keening. Her eyes puffy with tears, her whole being racked with terror, three months pregnant, she would not let go of him. Renowned for her beauty, she had grown even more winning during the first year of their marriage. Her skin, her laugh, her breath, her eyes – she was radiant while carrying her first child. During those months she was heavy and ripe and full of abandon, but after giving birth she grew weaker, plainer; she seldom spoke except to lash out at the servants. Two weeks before, weeping, she had followed her husband to the banks of the Danube to spend the nights before his departure with him. Leaving her two daughters in the village, she had moved to the reed-covered hut near the sty by the water to be with him on this last night. Lying for hours on his chest and whispering senseless, mindless nothings, she had covered his ribs, neck, eyes, mouth, and ears with kisses.

He, bowlegged and heavy, had spent the days riding and equipping his men. He cursed her hugs and kisses. She bored him.

Exhausted after quarrelling all day over the selection of men, who had arrived drunk and unarmed, he spent evenings with the clerks preparing the rolls of the Slavonian-Danubian Regiment. Then at night there was hell: her embraces, her insane attacks, her long, tireless fingers; her beauty, otherworldly by the fire, her eyes, her tears. His enormous chest, his enormous stomach, his low spirits, his concern for the children. He would cross himself in wonder at her madness – and laugh at it uproariously.

Gazing at her face still dazed with sleep in the candle's dim light, he knew that on this morning, the morning of his departure, she would be his greatest trial. The wild, frantic kisses falling over his face and neck were wet with tears. Rising to her feet the better to fling her arms around him, for he resisted her vehemently, trampling pillows, skins, and rugs scattered over the floor, she stepped on the frog with her bare foot and let out a terrified scream. Annoyed by her woman's frenzy, he pushed her away; he had half a mind to knock her to the floor. Overturning the bowl of holy water and basil she had prepared the night before, to sprinkle him when he awoke, staggering as if carrying an empty barrel over his head, he made his way to the door and threw it open.

It was drizzling. In the light of dawn he saw the dogs rushing up to him, the horses and servants under the mulberry trees, and, on the other side of the meadow, near the sty, the large crowd that had settled there the night before. The fires still painted the dark with elongated shadows and phantoms, but the moment the first shot was fired everyone seemed to be up

4

and milling about. Some began to sing and bellow, running to the well and the trough to wash; others, wrapping their infants in ragged swaddling, tried slipping down to the barges. Ah, how the women beat their breasts, wailed, and waved their white kerchiefs, sashes, foot cloths! Beyond the sty, beyond the hill, the grey rainy dawn was all willows and marshes as far as his eye could see, but there was no endless blue circle. Nor in it a star, as in his dream.

Running past the horses and weeping women, who were not allowed near the barges, the men converged with a shout. Some – stragglers, themselves in tears – were taking their leave and crossing themselves. One man approached him carrying an infant in his fur hat, looking for a hut with fire to provide shelter for the child, who was blue with cold. The dogs, in a pack, jumped up and down and splashed in the mud at the edge of the incline near the women and old men, barking at everyone who went down to the water.

Barefoot on the cold wet ground, wrapped in a ramskin he had slept under, but now wearing a tall black hat decorated with silver braid that he had stuck on his head the moment he leaped out of bed, he filled his servants with trepidation. They ran up to him, kissed his hand, and brought him a horse, which reared.

After several loud sneezes and some stamps of the foot that made the very ground shake, he withdrew into the dark to the heat of the fire, where his wife awaited him. She was still in tears. When he had finished washing, she dried his face with her hair, covering his cheeks with kisses, then dressed him quickly, kissing his greatcoat, his belt, his silver decorations. He took pity on her and stroked her back, but grumbled when her tears returned with increased vigour.

When he appeared again in the doorway, fully dressed, and the servants brought him his mount, there was such a din of keening and moaning among the womenfolk across the meadow, such a race to kiss his hand, that he roared at them.

While several servants on one side hoisted him into the saddle – the horse twisting and turning, frightened by all the noise and colour – two servants on the other side tightened the girth and secured the stirrups with their huge hairy hands. The horse sagged under him as under a full barrel.

Spattering the trees, grass, and dogs with mud, he guided the horse down the incline to the Danube. To escape the weeping and wailing, he made it trot through the wet trees and branches. The rain was nearly over, but the earth sank under the horse as they made their way downhill.

Day had dawned in the endless moisture of clouds and marshes, swamps and rushes. It was like another world, a world in which nothing happened – crows cawing above, light and dark patches of water sparkling below. The three barges, moored near a fire to old willow trees and stumps sticking out of the mud, looked black from a distance. Lifting his head, he saw the utter calm of the grey sky; he saw but could no longer hear the crows. He could see far down the Danube, along the banks – one rising high and yellow to the sky, the other, all floodwater and grass, sinking into the depths.

He emerged from the bushes into the marshland, his horse in mud to the fetlocks, just as the roasted lambs were being removed from the fire. The men had climbed into the broad boats, which were soaked from the bilge water. They spread out straw and dry yellow leaves to rest on, only to leap up again and clean their weapons or catch hunks of lamb with their knives, singing loudly.

Splashed with mud, he rode through the willows to the fire, where he met two officers and a priest. The priest had come with the man's brother all the way from the prosperous town of Zemun to take leave of his own son and bless the regiment. As he was intent upon setting off as soon as possible, he rode down to the moorings and gave the order for the barges to depart.

There was a minor commotion, the men jumping up to

catch one last glimpse of their loved ones. After the boatmen cast off, wading waist-deep through the water, shouting and pushing the boats away from the bank, the poor haulers, hired to drag a barge for a whole day, a whole night, and yet another day along the waterway, began to pull the ropes and wade through the mud. Two Gypsies among them, almost entirely naked, their chests wound round with rope, were gnawing some burned knuckles that no one else wanted to touch.

Old men, drenched and cold, stood motionless on the muddy bank while the women and children and dogs ran along the top of the steep incline, wailing and whimpering, until the barges were lost in the willows and all that was left was the men's hoarse song. As the people who had assembled to watch the barges began to disperse, the song faded away, little by little, until at last it was no more. The lamentations on the hill, however, trailed on.

The barges gone, the man rode his horse along the bank for a stretch, then urged the beast up the hill until it snorted and puffed wildly. He was returning to make ready his own departure.

A crowd had gathered near the stables and the sty to await his arrival, but even more to await the coach and horses and servants of his brother, Arandjel Isakovič, a merchant known throughout the Danube and Tisza basin for his wealth.

According to their agreement, his brother was to spend the night in the village with the children and rise early to be with him when he took leave of his wife, whose violent ways both men feared. And indeed, just as he reached the top of the hill, his brother's large brightly painted coach came into view and was immediately surrounded by servants.

By this time the rain had ceased, the sky had cleared.

Entering the hut, the man bumped his head on the thatched roof. He found his wife freshly washed, dressed in silk, beautiful. Tired from the strenuous ride, he looked at her in a new light. He went to her and started kissing her through

7

his bushy mustachio. In his haste he repeated, pell-mell and panting beneath her kisses, the words he had said to her the night before, the whole night before: instructions for her move to his brother's house in Zemun, advice for bathing their younger child, a girl with a skin condition; assurances that his journey through Styria and Bavaria would be a safe one, that the war would be brief and almost without incident, and that he would be faithful to her and return home. She, quaking like a madwoman, tore at her shining tresses, her buttons, the silk flowers and lace sewn on her dress, screaming the same words, the same supplications through her tears. Even while trying to resist her, and accidentally pulling her hair with the braid on his hat, he kept kissing her on the mouth, kissing her farewell, and repeating the sweet words she had so loved to hear during the first year of their marriage. Terrified, she hung on his neck, sprinkling him over and over with holy water and begging him not to marry there, as others did, not to try and distinguish himself, to send for her once he had arrived, to stay alive. She kissed him with a mouth she could no longer close or stop from trembling, gazed at him with eyes rolled upward, showing neither blue irises nor large pupils. Limp and only half conscious, she repeated convulsively, "I shall die! I shall die!"

Meanwhile, his brother, a man with dry sallow skin, had alighted from his coach wearing a long wolfskin coat and carrying an amber rosary like a cluster of large ripe grapes. He ordered the coach to be turned around, then dismissed the crowd graciously, giving a coin to whoever approached to kiss his hand. After exchanging several words with his servants, Arandjel gave a cheerful wave to the elder daughter, whom he had brought with him to take leave of her father and whom the servant would not let out of the coach.

The brothers had agreed upon a ruse, because the elder brother did not wish to see what his wife might do at the last moment. The younger brother was to bring the child in his coach to the hut near the sty, the sty where the men spent their last night before embarking for Varadin, the hut, used by shepherds in winter, where she had spent her last night with her husband. A servant had been told that as soon as the elder brother came out and jumped into the coach, he should whip the horses.

Everything happened in a flash. While she, more dead than alive, was adjusting her dress to appear in public with her husband, he, crossing himself in secret, rushed outside the minute he heard the whip crack, and found himself face to face with his brother. They quickly embraced, and he leaped into the coach, knocking the rosary into the mud.

Hearing the horses neigh and the crowd cheer, unsuspecting, she ran to the door just in time to see the coach disappear among the bushes and mulberry trees on the far side of the meadow. She collapsed, unconscious, into the arms of the younger brother.

Jolting off in the large, brightly painted coach, the weeping child in his arms, he rose just enough to see his wife faint. His head bent over the girl, he listened to the mud splash wildly as the coach swerved out of the way of branches, stumps, and ruts until at last the coachman came to a small locust grove and, leaning back hard, managed to rein in the three frightened and shuddering horses. Yelling orders to the servants and still embracing the child, the man felt for his weapon, greatcoat, boots, and brand-new silver-trimmed harness on the floor of the coach, and for the ducats, knife, and watch, round as an egg, in his belt. He had forgotten nothing.

Caressing his daughter, he ordered the coachman to drive slowly. Then, in full regalia, he started jumping and growling like an old bear. She petted him and tried to catch hold of the braid on his hat, laughing and crying.

The sky was clearing over the marshes and willows, the first larks chirping around the carriage. Flocks of crows swarmed over the horizon, its glittering broad expanses of floodland.

Following now the river, now the hills, which from time to time dipped into banks of wet grass, the coach soon caught up with the three large black barges moving slowly along the river below.

With the child's warm arms around his neck, he appeared to be sleeping. The trot of the hooves, the creak of the wheels, the voice of the child, along with the song of the larks and the caw of the crows, he experienced as a dream, which joined him to the rain clouds as they evaporated. Beyond them – far, far beyond them, but immense – was the sun.

The child, failing to receive an answer to each of her questions, repeated them a hundred times over, tugging at his ears, his facings, his mustachio. But weak and tired as she was, she eventually calmed down. He began to sing to her softly and rock her, and she laid her head on his breast and fell asleep.

Now that the rain was over, a warm spring day was in the making. A heavy mist rose over the marshes and willows on the far side of the river, and soon it rested on the river itself, thick and milky. By the time the song of the men in the barges drifted up to him, it was all but inaudible; it seemed to come from underground.

Above the purple hills and forests to his left he sensed the brightness of the fresh, sunny morning. He stopped the coach by a row of tall poplars. After covering the sleeping child with kisses, he left her in the coach and had the servants hoist him into his saddle. Then he rode off into the underbrush and waited serenely for the men to transfer his belongings from the coach to his other horses, moving back at one point so they could turn the coach around. After dismissing them, his brother's servants, he paused there for a while to watch the coach make its way back through the thick grass, and the larks fly out of the grass in front of the horses.

He took off his hat, gave it to his groom, and rode off, bouncing like a barrel.

He had done what needed doing. Back on his horse, his

daughter safely dispatched, he felt the full weight of the last few sleepless nights, all the preparations and riding, descend on him. The moist odour of the underbrush, the sultry heat of the low, sun-drenched clouds, the thick mist rising from the water stifled him, lulled him towards sleep. Before him lay not grief – he had left that at home – but the endless plain of thick grass that saps one's strength. Yet he was at peace: he had set off early and hoped to reach Varadin before dark, where a number of battalions were due to join his regiment. The men came from villages all over Slavonia and Srem, and under his command they would enter the town of Pécs, where he was to hold a review before setting off for the encampments of Charles of Lorraine, whose advance guard, under the command of Field Marshal Lieutenant Baron Johann-Leopold Bärenklau, had reached the Rhine.

Like his father, whose memory he evoked whenever he had something important to say, he went to war with a feeling of melancholy bordering on silence, and a melancholy that grew greater with age. He had had enough of migrations and the turbulence they brought to him and his men, having moved with his family from one town to another up and down the Danube and the Tisza and having engaged in commerce with his brother there until he married and returned to the military. He was highly regarded by the army and had been vouchsafed a number of important missions, often in regions where the people needed reassurance as a result of their constant migration.

He knew he would be sent into battle immediately after the review. Self-possessed and self-confident, he saw the whole road ahead of him: what would happen, how his men would behave. His only worry was that the battalion led by Captain Piščević from Šid would not arrive in Varadin on time.

Heavy with sleep, he rode through the grass with his head down. The hotter and clearer the sky, the heavier he felt. The horse's swaying gait completely debilitated him. What he had left behind seemed never to have been; his wife's tears, his brother's look, the warmth of the young child had merged with the mist. His mounted men trailed far behind him; he felt completely alone.

Riding on, pondering the disposition of his troops, all of whom, officers and men, he knew personally, he nearly dozed off. So, he thought, all one has to do is move away from a place and what one leaves behind appears never to have been. He gazed up into the distant hills, behind which the sun was beginning to show. Touched by its silver, he suddenly felt agile and light, bodiless. Thus transfixed by the sun, he no longer felt he was riding, no longer felt he existed in the invisible breeze that greeted his face.

He urged his horse into a trot. Through the void.

Thus did Vuk Isakovič set off for battle in the spring of the year 1744.

2

When They Left,
Nothing Remained Behind Them.
Nothing

They entered Pécs so unkempt, so unwashed, so wet and over-wrought that they made the children cry and the women, who had rushed out of their houses to see them, run off screaming in all directions. They sang at the top of their lungs and, exhausted and ravenous, marched with so impatient a step that, surrounded as they were by silver-trimmed officers, they looked like a pack of hungry hounds led on leashes to the hunt.

They struck fences with the butts of their rifles, beat dogs, tore trees out by the roots and tossed them into courtyards a few houses down the road. They whooped and gibed a herd of oxen into panic when they happened upon it around a corner.

They glutted the narrow alleyways of the lower town as they climbed. They spread out and lagged behind despite the shouts of the billeting officers, who had ridden out to meet them and assign them lodging. The musicians, who gathered around the large flag behind which the officers had ridden all the way from Varadin on skittish, foaming horses, were unable to overpower the singers, who roared "Hey . . . Hey . . ." in ever greater numbers, until it spread like a lament through the whole swarm, reaching even the stragglers, who, having waded knee-deep in mud and then fought over the first wells they came upon, were now racing through the streets, guided by the din of the regiment as it moved farther on through the town.

The Commissioner had spied them back at the first vine-yards, below the Bishop's gardens, and decided to quarter them outside the town, near the graveyard. He lured them there by means of a number of rams roasting over fires and a running drum-and-trumpet accompaniment. Through the falling dusk, Isakovič managed to lead them to a fenced-in meadow beyond which Turkish funeral monuments stood like old stumps with stone turbans in the grass. The meadow was immediately surrounded by Austrian artillerymen, who stood by their cannons late into the night with lit fuses close at hand.

Everything went well, however, once the men threw down their weapons and haversacks. The singing ceased and was immediately replaced by a general din. Calm was not restored until the officers dismounted and mingled with the men. Units began sorting themselves out while tents were being distributed near the fires, and by the time straw and wine were handed out, the men had found their sergeants.

They divided the camp in two, like a long village, with a straight path marked off by a series of small smoky fires kindled on damp young grass. As at home, they dug holes to lie in. Only then, to the steady accompaniment of the drummers, did they put up the tents.

Most of the men were young and off to war for the first time, though there were those among them who had seen battle on all sides the past few years, and those who had spilled their blood at Belgrade and Grocka, and even those who had, some thirty years before, mowed down the Turks at Varadin and Temesvár under Prince Eugene of Savoy.

Night fell here – below the steep paths of Pécs, in the deserted graveyard, in the meadow – as quickly as the misty grey evenings fell at home, sprinkling the marshes like rain, but here the spring evening fused the men in its endless blue. The blue slopes and forests above the evening mist were so sparse that the red of day still shone through. Above the forests, which surrounded them on all sides, were stars twinkling and endless crickets chirping. These were the first true hills they had climbed since arriving from the plain, and they found them disturbing. After nearly all the men had settled down in tents, in trenches, or on beds of straw, one after another they began lifting their heads.

Night fell over the camp.

The fires went out, but silence, silence for sleep, had not come. The strange sound of bells from the town invaded them. From the back streets, glimmering below the hill, a cacophony of barking, muffled music and a booming noise reached them. Then the few guards surrounding the camp with their cannons began calling out to one another. Most striking, from the hills came the fragrance of fruit trees; never had they seen so many fruit trees in one place before.

The quieter the camp became, however, the less desire they had to sleep. Though they were all tired and sore after six days of marching and toting heavy guns and packs, the only ones who slept were those who had been through it before and found nothing to marvel at: not the night beneath the dark, clear sky, not the fruit trees that made their presence so keenly felt in the darkness, not the barking of dogs that is everywhere the same, not the fire that makes the eyes water and the face turn black and warms one side while leaving the other to freeze.

The men who were on their first campaign began to rise to their knees and whisper, calling softly to one another and gathering like shadows behind the tents. Later the moon came out and lit up a broad swatch of land, and the boundless meadow beneath the dark hill suddenly appeared before them. They saw trees that had seemed empty darkness until then; they saw roofs in the town that had seemed sunk into the ground. And nearby, just beyond the fences separating them from the streets, they thought they saw a bevy of multicoloured feminine shadows strolling.

Arched high above them was the clear blue vault dotted

with clouds which became visible only as they sailed across the constellations. The grass growing up on the hillside that night, growing on the slopes to the horizon, filled the camp with an omnipresent murmur that circled each tent like so many mounds of earth dug soundlessly, invisibly, by a band of moles. Whispering in the silence, the shadows of the tents on their backs, the men began to crawl, more and more of them, through the grass, the darkness, the trenches, under the fences, out of the camp. Signalling to one another by soft whistling, half running, half slithering from hillock to hillock, from tree to tree, like squirrels, they managed to break through the cordon, confounding the guards, who, sensing something but at a loss to contain it, strained their eyes in the moonlight and took an occasional potshot into the night.

Before long a good half of them had thus made for the town through the dark. Since in the days immediately preceding their departure, amid the general howling and keening, they had had their fill of their women, of kissing them and beating them, they did not now go in search of carnal pleasure. Their limbs burning, their necks aflame from the long march and the weight of their equipment, they ventured into the night, all in wonder and marvelling at the proximity of so great and magnificent a town, which had passed so quickly before their eyes when they entered it at sunset. Knowing full well they would be unable to take trophies of glass or gold, of cows or calves, they were nevertheless dazzled by the many objects glittering in the night, beautiful and new to them; knowing that the most they could hope for was to find a wrinkled old crone, a wreath of onions, a halter, or a silver belt buckle, they went joyfully into the night to maraud.

After waiting in the ravines below the camp for three or four of their number to group together, they quickly asked what village each was from and what officer he was serving, and set forth through the bushes, following the leader, until they found a path. Most of them had never been in these parts before.

It was a night of miracles. Emerging from the bushes around the camp, they climbed the town's walls and crossed its gardens; they penetrated the town like wolves through its steep streets narrow and wet as gutters. Deserted as the streets were, the men could sense in the dark what they were after. They did not touch the chickens on the perches or the geese, but they grabbed as many doves as they could lay their hands on. Their shadows pinned by the moonlight to the walls, they plucked off the birds' blue heads and, fingers coated with sticky blood and feathers, felt the warm bodies twist and turn. They advanced on all fours through the moonlight, frightening dogs with their leaps and shadows. They stopped and stared through cracks at the strange faces in any house where a light was still burning, then wearily resumed their wandering.

They left, and they left nothing behind them. Nothing.

Some of them did break into houses. Staving in a door, they stood on the threshold and shouted a cheerful greeting that no one could understand. They strode up to the terrified occupants, stroked them, calmed them, guided them out of crannies and over to the fire with hands like shovels. And since they did not know their tongue, they spoke to them in growls, grumbles, roars, and neighs, a mixture of all the day and night sounds they knew from their own homes. They excelled in the wind's whistle, the horse's trot, and, most of all, the cock's crow. How they made themselves understood God only knows, but once they had gathered a family in front of the fire, they told stories, and the family members nodded approval. And thus having awakened the townspeople, they kept them up.

They went from house to house in the dark. Though not seeking women out, they happened upon them. After muffled cries and struggles they disappeared into the dark, and later they parted tenderly, lovingly, behind fences overgrown with thistles, near streams purling down the hillside. Sometimes a woman saw them off along the street, in the moonlight, all the way down to the meadow; sometimes a house they had left brightened the darkness with the light streaming through its wide-opened door.

Not everything ended happily, however. Some had turned malevolent, and, in two places, for no reason whatever, roaming through the dark, they set fire to roofs.

The moonlight, white as hoarfrost, shone brightest on the fruit trees, which grew more visible with the growing dark. Above the broad slopes, now crisscrossed by cuirassier guards with lanterns, and on the lookout for the runaways, rose a church with an enormous clock. Several of the soldiers had flattened themselves against the wall near the church to escape the patrol that had suddenly appeared in the deserted moonlit main square.

The enormous clock – its iron hands, its constantly scraping mechanism, its large incomprehensible ciphers painted around the white circle – cast a spell over them. Hidden in the dark, against the wall, they watched it chime the hour, its two metal weights swinging above their heads. They held their breath after the bells fell silent, and listened carefully. The moon lit up the large houses opposite the church, the walls and roofs of the lower town, and, in the distance, the woods and hills all the way to the sparkling deep sky.

Dejected, battered, so exhausted they had to sit and rest every few minutes, the men teetered back to camp half asleep. The cuirassier patrol notwithstanding, most made it back unapprehended; the only two picked up in town had been involved in a brawl. A few were found at daybreak in houses and stables; awakened from their drunken stupor, they grabbed their knives and charged after animals and people.

The last of them, Isakovič's orderly Arkadije, remained at large until broad daylight, when he was sighted in the vicinity of the camp with a sow tied to his foot. He was carrying on a gentle conversation with it, singing through his nose and hiccuping, all the long way from the inn in the lower town, where he had grabbed this prize, to the houses on the outskirts near the camp.

He appeared sober and content, and the people who had spent the night awake and in fear behind locked doors let him pass through the town, at a loss what to make of him. He maintained his serenity even when the guards surrounded him: he did not struggle or pay any attention. He was lazy, so lazy that he had let himself be jerked along by the sow. Suddenly the sow came to a halt; he tripped over it and fell – not because he was still drunk but because he had dozed off.

The next day was the day designated for the review.

The buglers and drummers woke the men at dawn. The sergeants kicked the heavier sleepers and overturned tents where necessary. Then they distributed tallow for greasing rifles, pistols, and knives.

Several hundred pipes were lit, several hundred moustaches waxed.

The men were damp with dew, bits of straw from the tents sticking out of their dishevelled hair. To the officers' horror they looked like Gypsies emerging from a caravan. No sooner did they start greasing their guns, powder flasks, ramrods, triggers, firing pins, barrels, and all the rest of those foul rusty parts that had to fit together, than the singers struck up their "Hey . . . Hey . . .," filling the camp with its plaintive, doleful sonority.

After greasing their belts, the men spread out their greatcoats and scraped the mud from them with their fingers. Then they combed their fur hats as if the hats were black sheep. They never noticed the mist-covered hilltops, the burgeoning forests, or the early-morning fragrance of the grass; they never noticed the first rays of light struggling to penetrate the foggy valleys to the east. Their legs swollen and aching, their will broken, utterly unmindful of their loved ones at home, unable even to talk or laugh, they ran to take their places, one behind the other, along the route the officers, cudgels in hand, would be taking.

Suddenly Captain Antonovič's horse bucked in the middle of the camp, and a number of men came running to bring it under control. Just then a coach full of plumes and white wigs appeared near the houses at the edge of town. The Governor's officers had arrived. The drums rolled, and a mad rush followed along the piles of ashes and smoking coals. The men pulled to attention, threw out their chests.

The officers had brought three flags. One, the imperial flag, was very large and decorated, like the cuirassiers, with silk sashes, ribbons, and tassels.

In front of the camp they spread out large scrolls on a long table. That the scrolls included not only their own names, but the names of their fathers, wives, and children as well, always amazed and dismayed the men.

Meanwhile, a report on the exploits of the pandours was being made in the Governor's residence, where the commander of the regiment had spent the night. The paved baroque courtyard teemed with servants readying the horses and the large ceremonial coach, with tradesmen and artisans reporting their losses, and with whole families from the lower town submitting sundry complaints. Women had brought their crying children, men their aging fathers, to bear witness. The whole house was buzzing with talk about thefts, fires, brawls, and an instance of rape.

Still in his nightclothes, the Governor appeared shouting, in a second-storey window. Vuk Isakovič – with a soldier pouring water over him, washing his hair – was visible in another window of the old building.

Upon wakening, the Most Honourable Isakovič had been surprised by the pictures above his head, the clock that insisted, despite his imprecations, on playing a minuet for him, and numerous spindly-legged tables and silk coverlets, one with two white cats sleeping on it.

Having been designated the Colonel's replacement, he knew he would be named lieutenant colonel here. So it meant a great deal to him that everything should proceed properly, all the more so as the Governor had failed to bring up the promotion the night before. Instead the Governor had spent half the night harping on the follies committed by Lieutenant Colonel Arsenije Vuič and the damage caused by the coastal border guards led by Ivan Horvat. Isakovič had found the Governor and the entire evening highly irritating.

Bathed and shaved, he stood before the large mirror in his room and, while keeping an eye on what was happening in the courtyard, examined first the broad scar on his right shoulder, then his large, sagging cheeks. Although he wished to hurry, needed to hurry, he went through many unnecessary motions and interrupted his toilet with long pauses at the mirror, the likes of which he had not seen at home. His chest and legs, his puffy eyes, yellow and spotted, and especially his stomach, looked ridiculous and alien to him in the mirror, and struggling into his red uniform, he had the feeling that he was watching someone else being dressed, that someone else would now leave the room in his regimentals.

Just before dawn he had dreamed of his wife, and he thought of her now, as he stood at the misty window watching his horse's pasterns and thin hocks being washed by his men. Recalling the children, he burst into muffled sobs, right in front of the soldier who was dressing him. The call to arms – it had come so abruptly – had thwarted all his plans. Having quarrelled with his brother, who was living in Zemun but eventually intended that they buy a large house in Buda together, Isakovič had hoped to withdraw his seven hundred ducats from the deal and move to Russia, which he imagined as an endless green meadow made for him to ride across.

His children were constantly ill; the youngest was plagued with boils. Yet he, heavy, turgid, barrel-like as he was, had felt light as a feather the moment the call to arms arrived. Not that it was the first time he had trudged up and down the Rhine; indeed, he had nearly had his head cut off in a skirmish near a tributary of the Danube. From there he had been sent to Italy, even though he was married and a father and showed no desire whatever to go. In an attempt to leave the military, he started transporting grain, he settled in Galatz, on the Lower Danube, and sent barges up to Vienna, but he soon lost what fortune he had. His land, his livestock, his children's ailments and tears – they were not taken into account: he was continually forced to pick up and move on.

It had been the same when he was a child: the family would find a place near the water, a quiet place with a mild summer, lush fruit trees, and good people, but no sooner was winter over than off they went. Then his father died, and he wanted to settle down. He felt a curious connection with his dead father, a kind of peace and tranquillity, while everything around him, everything in the world, was tumult, bedlam, folly, nonsense.

As for the living, his wife and, even more, his children, whom he loved, were constantly having to move, from spring to autumn, summer to winter, day to night, from joy to tears. Although he had charge of them, he could not help them; he could not even keep them with him. The first time he left, he found them a large yellow Turkish house surrounded by poplars, high on the banks of the Danube, above a spot where smugglers moored their boats. The second time, he found them a low-roofed inn outside Vienna. The third time – two years ago, after the younger girl was born – he found them the house of a Greek at Slavonski Brod, where they spent the winter, awaiting the return of his brother, who had gone to Venice on business. He had seen the house for only a few moments – and in the dark at that – and remembered nothing of it, though he did recall a gap-toothed woman sobbing violently as he took leave of his wife. This time he pictured his family in his brother's house, a large timber-beamed structure on the Danube at Zemun with brightly painted multicoloured boats gliding by like so many crook-necked, potbellied swans. He had no idea what would become of him. He had no idea whether he would see them again.

Drained by the pain in his knee that he had tried to ignore, he sat still, unable to finish dressing and strap on his weapons.

Other thoughts kept coming to him. Just as he cared for his wife and children, he cared for his men, his churches, all his people, who knew neither where they were going nor what they wished to find. Relations with the local clergy (the quarrels had been particularly violent that winter), the construction of a church he had undertaken in the village, the stand of trees he had cleared on the island, leaving huge rocklike stumps – everything seemed to be going against his wish and will. Shortly before this call to arms he had been summoned to the Imperial Court in Vienna with a group of monks, and the confusion and depravity he had seen there were beyond belief!

Only the mausoleum marking his father's resting place stood immutable and plain to see at the top of the hill, high above the grass and the wheat that had begun to bud and bear in the last few years. Three poplars quivered nearby in the wind; he could see them clearly no matter what the distance. The wisdom and peace, the tranquillity that filled his soul came from there and accompanied him in his travels as if he were merely making the rounds of the wheat fields with his greyhounds. And when everything spun around him in disarray, disorder, and confusion, the thought of his father would find him on a hillside, in a spring landscape, or, as now, over the roofs of a town, and would put everything back in place, restore order, return peace.

All puffed up beneath his feathers like a turkey, red of face and neck, the Governor went from room to room, up and down the stairs, and through the courtyard, screaming at his officers, trying to settle what he could, releasing those in chains and having those who were still drunk doused in a barrel of water until they choked. When estimating damages, he capriciously doubled, halved, or cancelled the amounts due, and refused outright to deal with the women and old men, telling them to go and make their complaints to God. As for the single instance of rape, he was inclined to dismiss it: he had expected many more.

He soon cleared the baroque courtyard of all petitioners and jumped into the coach, magnificently fitted out for the occasion, asking for the third time whether anyone knew where the commander, Isakovič, was. He jumped down again and started waving his arms in the direction of a large window, above which, among the ivy, several naked female figures were sitting in the company of demigods draped in garlands of baked clay overrun by sparrows.

All that time the guard at the door – frightened, his rifle pressed to his bulging chest – stood stiff and still, or rocked slowly on his heels.

Since the Governor could not stop thinking about the speech he had to give, he kept taking from his pocket a large envelope covered with big red seals and containing the instructions for dispatching the troops, which had come from Cavalry General and Inspector of the Field Army Count Serbelloni. The Governor had used it to write out the opening sentence of his speech: "You Serbs have always been partial to the military, and therefore . . ."

Distressed that he had forgotten the rest of the speech, he repeated the sentence – in German, of course – to everyone he encountered that morning. He could not get past it. The only Serbian he really knew consisted of curses, and he used them freely in his orders to the officers. Since he was distracted, however, after each curse he would say to his adjutant, who was never more than a step to the right or left of him, "Auersperg, tell them that in Serbian."

Isakovič trotted up at last, out of breath, and he and the Governor, both mortified and angry, took their places in the coach, which set off, accompanied by a cortège of officers on horseback. They exchanged not a word during the trip except when the Governor recited the first sentence of his speech, only to confirm that he could recall no more of it. Isakovič was angry because he feared the foolish old hag in military dress, and the Governor was angry because Isakovič's weight tilted the coach to the left and forced him to sit at an angle.

They were welcomed by flags, shouted commands, salvos, salutations, and reports. The sun had been unable to break through the clouds. It was a warm, murky morning.

Alighting from the coach, the Governor looked up, as though to judge the probability of rain, then stood before the troops. They were trembling with fear. Trembling with fear himself, he shouted, "You Serbs have always been partial to the military, and therefore . . ." He could go no further.

To cover up, he quickly read out a rescript from the commander of Osijek, the Marquis Guadagni, and began the review.

Surrounded by a crowd of his German officers and sweating profusely, he personally inspected man after man, rifle after rifle, pistol after pistol, inserting his little finger into the muzzles for dust, yet careful to deflect all barrels that happened to point at his chest. He verified each entry in the records, inspected hair, legs, knives. After a while he unbuckled his sword and, as his humour improved, started turning to his officers and commenting, "What men! What hairy men!"

Hundreds of men and thousands of belts, pistols, and buckles thus passed before his eyes and through his hands. He sent some of the men to the blacksmiths, others to the gunsmiths, still others to the saddlers, and kept those he wished to reward by his side. He was content: he had found more than a hundred capable of pronouncing "Maria Theresa" clearly and correctly and adding *"vivat"*; he had even found some who could salute on the march without halting. He thus considered the regiment first-rate, and as he had been instructed to be lenient, he decided to draw a veil over the incidents of the previous night.

He had a passion for administering discipline at a distance. He delighted in sending a regiment on its way and then issuing a dispatch, written in his clear, needle-sharp hand, that required others to mete out the punishment. This time, however, he tempered his bile and turned, all rosy and dripping with sweat from his white wig, to the officers and, after draping one of his large gloves over his belt and looking each of them – stiff, bareheaded, immobile – up and down, said through his teeth in an amiable, slightly absentminded way, gazing off above the town, above the church tower, to a flock of doves, "Congratulations, Herr Isakovič, especially on the arms, though the forage is admirable as well. I hereby revoke all punishments for last night's incidents – all but one, that is. The rapist shall run the gauntlet – the gauntlet of the entire regiment."

Thus it came about that the Slavonian-Danubian Regiment would spill blood before it ever reached the Rhine, human blood, its own.

After a brief, uncomfortable silence that ran through the entire regiment like a shudder, commands began to fly, and the regiment laid down its arms and was led off, away from the camp, to carry out the punishment and remember the night of plunder, drunken revelry, and lechery.

Having been divided into two lines, as on festive occasions, they were given hard rods, wet and shiny, that whistled in the air. Heads down, they planted their feet firmly, mutely straightening their ranks. Casting furtive glances right and left, they saw two rows of enormous feet that seemed to stretch to the end of the earth in which they were rooted.

Meanwhile, the victim had been bound above the ankles

and elbows and tossed down at the entrance to that curious path he would be forced to walk, which was lined not with trees but with his fellow countrymen, who had suddenly grown branches. Trussed and panting, he waited for the ordeal to begin, shuddering occasionally like the rams that had lain there the previous night before their slaughter.

While his sentence was read aloud – beneath the flag, to the beating of drums – from a parchment decorated with large red seals – the victim lay on the ground, his knees bent, his face as dark as the earth. The reading over, the officers placed their hats back on their heads and mounted their horses.

Bloated with impotent rage, Isakovič called for the field doctor and a cart for the man to be loaded on afterwards, like carrion. He had recognized him as one of his own soldiers, for he knew them all. Horrified by the thought that the miserable creature might be blind and paralysed within a few minutes, he rode closer and leaned down so far from the saddle that he nearly threw his horse off balance. The man was a former sexton from his village and he was crying. Isakovič said, softly, moved by something deep within, "Forgive me, Sekula, but what am I to do in my great perplexity? Judge for yourself: are my hands not also tied? Therefore do not weep. Shall I and my regiment find the way to the Virgin of the Shining Countenance? No, my long life will pass like a brief one, for wherever I go I see only the gall of death."

Naked to the waist, the man had been carried to the banks of a stream along which his body would now float as through a meadow overhung with willows. Then his legs were unbound and his mouth was freed of the gag, and he stood and moaned, as if feeling the blows. No pity was forthcoming: he was immediately pushed from behind into the space between the rows of soldiers.

The first one gave him an awkward blow on the head. The rod grazed the skin, but only a thin thread of blood appeared on the man's forehead.

The drums began to roll.

For a moment he merely stood there, his eyes bulging, then another soldier lashed him squarely in the face, splitting a lip and causing the blood to gush forth. Only then did he begin to run. He was overwhelmed by blows to his head, neck, chest, and back. Howling with pain, his arms still bound, the blood streaming down his face, he made little progress, swerving, swaying, teetering in such a way that from a distance, from the coach, where the Governor and his cuirassiers were watching, he looked like a giant flower – now white, now red – waving in the wind.

The first time he fell, they poured water over him and prodded him on. The water splashing in his face and over his head and chest restored his sight and strength for an instant, and he set off running again like a madman, his ears drooping red and bloody like the gills of a fish.

Again he fell, awash in blood, his arms tangling in the soldiers' legs. By then his nostrils were slit and his hands and fingers were broken and dangling like ragged sleeves.

Waving his bound wrists in the air, trying to shelter eyes that no longer saw, he staggered, wobbled, crawled his way on, crisscrossed by rills of blood.

In their haste and revulsion the two rows of soldiers started lashing at each other, meeting in a snarl over the man each time he stumbled. The skin on his neck and shoulders was torn, chunks of flesh burst forth like choice morsels.

He lost consciousness, but revived more than once, writhing on the grass in pain.

Once it was over – the entire process had taken no more than a few minutes – the field doctor set to washing the man's face. He could not distinguish nose, mouth, eyes, or ears. The man's own mother would not have recognized him.

The regiment returned to the camp. Reinforcements were ordered for the guard within the camp and around it.

As word of the ordeal reached the town, the inhabitants

were seized by fear. They retreated to their houses early in the evening, bolting all doors. By the time the moon came out, they were trembling. The evening passed without incident, however, and the regiment whimpered and howled through the night like so many beaten dogs.

The regiment was due to break camp at dawn. Its next stop was the town of Radkersburg.

That evening the officers were invited to the castle of the Bishop of Pécs, who knew the language of the regiment because his flock included thousands of Catholic Slavs.

Obliged to spend the entire day with the Governor, Isakovič had left Captain Piščevič, from Šid, in command. The other officers waited now for Isakovič in front of a castle gate over which a band of angels held the Bishop's coat of arms. The fragrance of lilacs and the glow of a lantern streamed out of nowhere. A huge spider was making its way down from its web on one of the angels, but the men failed to notice it above their jaunty black three-cornered hats.

When the time came, they entered the courtyard without Isakovič and were immediately ushered into the Bishop's chapel to attend the Mass being said for "the long life and military victory" of Maria Theresa. Dashing in their bright red, silver-trimmed uniforms and long hair, they crossed themselves with three fingers and exchanged bewildered glances when the Bishop blessed them and sang a nasal *Dominus vobiscum*. They were enraptured by the heavenly music emanating from the organ and choir, the aroma of incense, the jumble of Latin, the angelic expressions on the faces of the Bishop's altar boys.

First they sat on the benches illuminated with muted, multicoloured patterns from the stained glass; then, their swords clanking, they fell to their knees under the spell of the magnificent atmosphere: the dignified demeanour of the priests, the frequent genuflections before the gold chalice, the faces of the fair-haired boys, the heavenly radiance filtering through the windows. They remembered their own quaint wooden churches, in which people not only sang loudly but spat loudly, and their wild and wanton priests, and, though they tried to hide it from one another, they grew forlorn, though they admired, breathed in the soaring, luminous Catholic cantilenas, the exquisite string accompaniment, the intricate Roman rite as performed by the priests and their Bishop under a canopy of red and gold.

By the end of the service they were so exhausted that they exchanged not a word. One after the other they kissed the Bishop's ring, and ghostlike they crossed the courtyard to the brightly lit stairway leading into the castle. Next to the main hall, where a large table was being set for a banquet, they found a room with walls covered entirely in red silk, and there they waited for Isakovič, who was so long in coming that when he did arrive they were surprised.

His face was ashen, yet he was all blue silk ribbons and sashes beneath his white-plumed tricorn. He looked like a straw-stuffed monster. His trousers stretched tight when he sat, but hung like a sack when he stood. His skin was flaccid, his greying yellowish hair bristly, his mustachio unkempt and twitching. His eyes rolled, bulged, wandered. Who could tell where he wanted to go, or what his twisted lips wanted to say? In his bloated face, still twinging with fury and despair, only the large flat nose was peaceful, immobile. Two big tears ran down his cheeks.

In vain did the officers rush to console him, in vain did they lay him, like a log, on a couch by the wall: he continued to breathe heavily. Aware that he suffered from asthma and various stomach ailments, they loosened his belt and unbuttoned his shirt where the thick, grasslike, sweat-drenched hair on his chest invaded the lace. Clutching his stomach convulsively, he rocked back and forth.

When the servants came to escort them to the main hall and

their places at the sumptuous board, Isakovič gave a start and with bearlike tenacity pulled himself to his feet. His eyelids were blue. He motioned to them to go in and said softly, "Go and be not offended by my weakness. You have no need of vain words from me. Pay tribute to the Empress, yet keep in your hearts our silent hope: sweet Orthodoxy."

And when he saw the bewildered expression on their faces, he again motioned to them to go in and again pronounced his final words, but more softly: "Sweet Orthodoxy."

What the officers did not know was that the distinguished Major and commander of the Slavonian-Danubian Regiment, Vuk Isakovič, had spent the day in Pécs wedged between the Bishop's enormous faience bowls and Venetian glassware, which he had to take care not to break, and the Governor, who was by then half asleep and half drunk and even more bedecked than he in sashes and silk ribbons and plumes, which he had to take care not to crush. And he was forced to discuss heaven and hell and angels and archangels, for they had taken it into their heads to convert him to Catholicism.

The Governor had a passion for committing his successes to paper. He dreamed of putting into words – or, rather, into fine, pointy script – the fact that upon the departure of the elite battalions of the Slavonian-Danubian Regiment, its commander, Vuk Isakovič, one of the finest officers in the Governor's territory, enlightened by the divinely inspired words of the Bishop of Pécs, had bowed and kissed the Holy Father's slipper, thus going forth from the Military Frontier a true believer – and *eo ipso* greater hero – to the wars on the Rhine.

While making no mention of Isakovič's promotion to the rank of lieutenant colonel, the Governor had gone on and on about the Empress, the Court, and Vienna, his goal being to make it crystal clear to Isakovič that he had no choice but to become a Catholic.

Sitting between two six-taper candelabra, beneath a

painting of Saint Catherine of Siena with stigmata, her eyes raised to the sky, the Governor came at last to the end of his harangue. He had harangued all day and decided the time had come to hand the matter over to the Bishop. The wine and the heavy wig had worn him out; his lower lip was drooping, his face had lost its colour, he looked like an old woman suffering from heartburn. He started composing in his mind the report of his failure. He pictured it as a general statement, in his usual fine, pointy letters, a description of "Orthodoxy in the Military Frontiers". Muddled as he was, he could go no farther than the first sentence: "Serbs have always been partial to the military, and therefore . . ." As he gave up trying to think, Isaković turned a leaden blue, more a picture than a man.

By now the Governor was all but motionless. Only his eyes blinked. At home it was evening, he thought. Both cats must be asleep. He stroked his aquiline nose with his index finger, wondering how the Bishop would handle it. Two documents had to be prepared for the General, Count Serbelloni, the next day. This was the night they would give him a clean nightshirt. How very pleasant!

The walls were covered with yellow brocade. Besides the Catherine of Siena there was a Saint Theresa and, in a corner, a Maria with a handsome bare leg resting on the serpent and the moon.

The veins in his hands! Bad wine. He opened his mouth to call for Auersperg, but the adjutant was nowhere in sight. Music from the dining room wafted through the open door, mixing with the scent of lilacs. He took to counting the candles. Once he got to eleven, he could go no further.

The Bishop, always calm and smiling, had faith in the Divine Will. He had ordered a table set for three in a room above the chapel in the southern wing of the castle, the room he gave to his sister and the occasional aunt when they came to visit. The room had a fragrance all its own and, on the ceiling, an unusually large number of angels. It also had a fine view of the surrounding hills.

It was there he had brought Isakovič and the Governor to dine, supplementing each course with an abundance of wines as old as the boys in his choir. And he let them wear themselves out arguing about church rites, patriarchs, Holy Communion, baptism, and the Resurrection. Not that either of them had anything intelligent to say. How little they understood the Roman church!

He had the door opened wide to let in the scent of the lilacs, acacias, and chestnut trees, the view of blue hills and glittering stars, and, tilting his head slightly to catch the strains of music from the main hall, he began to expatiate on how tender and compassionate the Catholic church was. Without saying directly what Isakovič could gain by it, the Bishop urged him to consider, with his officers, the harm that evil men who hated the Orthodox schismatics, men whom he knew to be prevalent at Court, might cause their families. From time to time he placed his soft white hand with its dazzling black ring on the hand of the now quite intoxicated Isakovič.

Thus, at the far end of the dark castle grounds, in a wing of the old building with large brightly lit windows crisscrossed by black bars and shadows, the two men remained locked in battle far into the night. Enclosed by yellow walls, bent over a table groaning with food and drink, they felt bloated and tired, and their words, their murmurs, their shouts penetrated deeper and deeper into the surrounding darkness – the woods, the hills, the endless starry sky glittering above the town.

Isakovič simply had to convert. How could a non-Catholic serve a Catholic Empress? The beautiful Empress, who united two peerless names: Maria and Theresa. Maria! The pure, the innocent Maria, the fair-haired shrine, the morning star. Maria the Miracle, the Mother. Did Isakovič know – did any of his people know? – and worship Saint Theresa?

33

Theresa! A fire! A ring that girded your body like a ring of the sun. A flame that set you burning for another life, more beautiful and sweeter. Theresa – her white breast untouched by the hand of man yet pierced by his sword. And the radiance! It was Isakovič's duty to lead his people to the light, to the radiance and light of Catholicism. The instant the sun set in the West, it appeared in the East. In Catholicism. What soldiers could they be if they were schismatics in the eyes of their Empress? How could they possibly bear the endless suffering, the endless migration of their souls and the souls of their children, the eternal change that, like lime in the grave, would gnaw at their flesh and bones as long as they remained of this land, which would not let them go?

Maria: the first letter of her name had a secret meaning, for M signified a thousand yet also Mother, A was for Angelic, R for Radiant in Knowledge, I for Immaculate, A for Angelic, again.

Likewise Theresa: T was for Theodicean, H for Holy, E for Evangelical, R for even more Radiant in Knowledge because she radiated so much, E for Ecstatic, S for Saintly, A for Apostolic.

Isakovič, who after dinner felt the usual pain stirring in his entrails, was sorely afflicted by the Bishop's words. Desperate at the thought that he would be unable to escape baptism here in Pécs, he invoked the aid of the family's patron saint, Mrata. And Saint Mrata came to his aid: in the midst of all the wine and flickering candles he suddenly recalled his brother, Arandjel, whose custom it was, while travelling on business through Walachia, Turkey, and Hungary, to ply his clients with drink, and with Arandjel in mind the much-esteemed Vuk Isakovič resolved to down so much drink that if in fact they did force him to convert, they would at least fail to convert him sober.

He set to drinking voraciously. The Bishop was so surprised, he fell silent. And Isakovič, in his final moments of lucidity, proved he did not need the aid of Saint Mrata for long by saying, "Just as my sweet Orthodoxy did reside forever within my mother, so shall it reside forever within me and those who come after me. Our Russia is also sweet. I pray to God the Creator to show me the way there. Russia! R for the Resurrection, U for the Universe, S for the Slavs, S for Salvation, I for the Immortality of Christ, A for . . ."

Intoxicated as he was, he held his tongue, afraid of saying what should not be said. Partly from fear, partly from sadness, he tried to cover up his words, deny them, for is not all dust and death and vanity, vanity of vanities . . . empty phrases? And when a man dies, does he not die as does the dog and the horse? At the same time, he tried to stand and leave. There is no soul . . . nor is there a God . . . vanity of vanities . . . dust . . . death . . . empty phrases.

The Bishop turned his cold eyes away and gazed into the night with a shudder. Midnight was long gone.

"Standing here, looking out into the night, gazing on the fields or the hills in the distance . . . the town, the roofs . . . the clouds . . . the constellations . . . the sky so full of light – is our passage through them meaningless, absurd? Can it all be nothing more than a bottomless void?"

Then the much-esteemed Vuk Isakovič roused the Governor and, completely inebriated, stared again into the star-studded night, letting his eyes wander across the moonlit fields, the woods, the hills, the clouds. And when his eyes came to rest on the Bishop's face, he whispered, "I pray to God the Creator to show me the way." And he burst into tears.

3

Day and Night, Broad and Stagnant,
the River Flowed. And in It
Her Shadow

The house of Arandjel Isakovič, a large structure at the edge
of the rich town of Zemun, had been newly roughcast in the
spring of 1744. Blue and yellow, rising high above the neighbouring stork-infested straw roofs, it was visible through the
willows far and wide, and all the fishermen and boatmen knew
it.

From the foot of the hill ravaged by spring, early sprouts,
and moles, the house seemed to be thrust into the bank of the
Danube amid a flock of brightly painted swans – boats with
high curved bows. Its raftered roof, taken from a barn, domi-
nated, like the Ark before the Flood, the surrounding stables
and sties, from which came the muffled roar of bulls and cows,
the stamping of horses and camels, the bleating of sheep and
goats.

Behind a fence where men waded from morning to night
through deep mud loading barges, Arandjel Isakovič had
hidden the remains of the treasure his forefathers brought
with them when they left the purple slopes of Macedonia and
the meadows of the Vardar valley.

On one side, the horizon was all water and misty islands, the
minarets and ramparts of Belgrade towering white beyond; on
the other, the water merged with a sea of mud stretching to
the ends of the earth beneath the deep blue sky. The house

was bordered by deep ditches and by stacks of fodder, whose fragrance spread in the still-sunny evening and penetrated not only the sparkling air but also the hot walls. Despite the uninterrupted din and bedlam of shepherds and boatmen, despite the daily roar of cattle and other animals and their keepers, the house remained quiet. Its walls were well insulated by plaster, and it had but a single low entryway, full of doves and with skins hanging from rafters. At nightfall, when boats glided by and fires were lit, it too looked like a boat, a ship stranded in the mud.

This was the house in which Vuk Isakovič had chosen to lodge his wife and two girls, who arrived in a coach loaded down with clothes, furs, carpets, pearl brooches, silver buttons, and the like, and accompanied by a crowd of loudly lamenting women and aging servants.

Though younger than his brother, Arandjel Isakovič treated Vuk as if he were the younger. Whenever he stood next to him, he gave him pitying looks; whenever he sat next to him, he made sure Vuk had the more comfortable seat, though he himself was thin as a rail and his brother round as a barrel; and whenever his brother spoke to him, he smiled, avoided his glance, and paused before responding.

While Vuk was in the service of Prince Alexander of Württemberg in Belgrade, Arandjel saw to his debts after card games, to his release from jail after brawls, and to his wounds and illnesses after wars. Tagging after his father, who followed the armies to Constantinople and Vienna, Arandjel had begun by trading in wheat, cattle, and tobacco, but as the years passed he dealt more and more in silver, lending money to anyone, until, running through the names of his debtors as he fell asleep at night, he was unable to calculate the total sum owed him. Travelling through Walachia or Turkey, among merchants sporting fezzes and fingering worry beads, he would think of his uniformed brother as just another oddly dressed debtor.

He had tried to turn Vuk away from the military and teach him his trade, but Vuk went right back to his horses and swords. After their father's death, when they spent a great deal of time together, Vuk had been a great trial to him: he had turned into a terrible drunkard, profligate, and brawler. It was then that he grew round as a barrel.

And so Arandjel had married Vuk off, going all the way to Vienna for permission and bribing half the fortress at Osijek to drag him, kicking and screaming, to the altar. He had found the girl, almost by chance, while doing business in Trieste with a family named Christodoulos which owed him eight thousand silver crowns. They soon came to an agreement. Arandjel found the girl to his liking because she was tall, young, and healthy, and because she stared out at the world with big, blue, stubbornly mute eyes.

While en route from one transaction to another, he saw them married in Slavonski Brod, at the house of a Greek friend. Then he sent them up and down the Danube, at his expense, as he did his cattle, and only when he heard that his sister-in-law was about to give birth did his pride in his ancestors, the Isakovičes, compel him to go and see them, exhausted as he was from the travel, trade, and villainies to which he had had to inure himself. It was only when he saw her with child that he really saw the woman he had chosen for his brother.

Strong and straight-backed like an angel, long-legged and possessing breasts and thighs that shook at her every step, she walked straight past him as he disembarked from the boat, walked as though to demonstrate that she was hard as stone yet no less supple for it. He felt he had never known such a woman.

Several days later he left his brother's house in a great hurry, and it was not easy for him later to return. He avoided them as the devil the Cross, though he kept sending them gifts of silver, silk, and coral. When he felt obliged to visit them, he left as quickly as he could. Living far from them, he grew old before his time – his skin dry and sallow, his knees stiff. He did most of his business on the water and travelled everywhere by boat, sitting motionless, deep in thought. Within a few years his shoulders were stooped, his fingers beginning to tremble.

Tormented, he dreamed of her night after night.

He saw her in the dark, wherever he was. He felt her hair wind around him, redolent of walnuts, light as silk. Her hair had grazed him several times when she approached to kiss his hand; he had grazed her hair several times himself. And each time, he sank his nails into the tobacco he had dried in the sun or by the fire.

In her absence he would picture her high forehead and leeches, as the brothers called her eyebrows because of their shape. In her presence he would forget himself and stare at her always pale face, her slightly protruding lips and long lashes, beneath which was darkness. He would wait for hours, on the flimsiest of pretexts, merely to see her retire to her bedchamber, tired of smoke and coffee. He would watch her straighten her broad back and pull in her stomach while removing two large pearls from her ears. It sent a shudder through his body.

No sooner did he close his eyes than he saw her white skin and her breasts and her large eyes, their blue the blue of a clear winter evening sky and never, when trained upon him, the least bit clouded.

Fleeing her the first year, he might have been fleeing a disaster, muttering, "Get thee behind me, misfortune!" Just as he avoided wild horses and heavy wines, just as he had once decamped from a caravanserai in Brusa, so did he flee his brother's house. There could be no thought of his absconding with his brother's wife. Yet how could he have brought her to *him*? Those extraordinarily powerful legs, that sway, that laugh. At first he feared for his brother: he had brought a devil into his house. Those quivering breasts, those strong thighs, those deep breaths she took when smoking. Contemplating her groin, the undulations of her body under her silk wrap as she slept, he compared her in his memory with the Walachian, Italian, and Armenian women he had had in the course of his travels. He greatly feared that she would consent to sin with him, there, at night, in his brother's house, at his brother's side, in exchange for gifts of beads and pearls. He greatly feared that he would catch her with a servant, a boatman, anyone. And he fled.

But when he returned and saw her with her child, he nearly cried, so great was the serenity in her eyes and the purity in her hands and neck. Taking pity on himself, he told her, in jest, innocently, what her life would be like were she his. He told her how he would look after her, how he would dress her, that he would take her everywhere with him. Life was beautiful, he felt, and he would make life beautiful for her and her child wherever they went. Kissing the child, he thought of the hundreds and hundreds of little Walachians, Germans, and Hungarians whose fathers he had fleeced, and he decided that much as he had tortured his clients in the past – and much as he had enjoyed doing so – he would now leave them in peace, for he pictured them now with their wives and children. It was then that he dared touch her for the first time. He stroked her unplaited hair; he kissed her on the cheek; he gazed into her eyes, pressing her strong shoulders, helping her to button her dress, though she had not asked him to. He would sit for hours with her, playing with the child or with the dogs, but devouring her with his eyes the while. Never for a moment did it occur to him to desire his brother's wife; on the contrary, he considered his brother a happy man and his own love for this woman, though incomprehensible to others, utterly pure. He lived only for them, neglecting his business endeavours in the hope of finding a way for them all to settle together in one place.

He realized his brother's happiness was the result of chance, but that was as it had to be. He could have turned the chance to his own benefit, but as he had not, she was not his. Free of rancour or despair, he stayed on in their household until the first days of spring. Then he drove along the flooded roads in his coach to inspect the walls of the church his brother had begun to build in the village settled by their father. He took care of the ecclesiastical matters in which his brother had involved him – and returned home with a kiss for her and for the child as if they were both his. Perfectly happy, he would ride out into the wheat, which was beginning to ripen in the muddy lowlands, or take a boat all the way to Buda, thinking of her, watching the birds, and enjoying the sun on his back.

Yet after those tranquil days in the shade of white acacias, unwittingly he began to do evil in his brother's house. More and more often he would touch his sister-in-law's hands, hair, shoulders, even waist; more and more often he would go up to her and breathe in the fragrance of the lace at her neck or help her, though there were all those servants to do the work, to tuck in the child at night or dress it in the morning. His brother, who spent much of his time at Varadin training his soldiers in the art of trench- and ditch-digging or at the arsenal in far-off Mitrovica, noticed nothing. And what she noticed, what she thought, was apparent neither in her face nor in her eyes. It was not until Holy Week – when he arrived home as she was bathing in the room with the large clay stove used for baking bread, and thought of entering – that he suddenly understood what it was he wanted. He left without a farewell, and did not return, or even pay a visit, for a long time, his brother's pleas notwithstanding.

Arandjel maintained his distance until she gave birth to a second daughter and his brother was about to leave for Italy with his troops. Arandjel joined the family in Vienna, where they were staying at a small inn nestled in an orchard. Vuk was still robust and handsome, though heavy and completely grey, and she loved him with a fervour Arandjel found both animal-like and repulsive. They embraced and kissed in front of him; they could not keep their hands off each other. All through the night, each time the child awoke and cried, he heard them whispering and cooing. Although he found her more beautiful than ever, she no longer roused him with her walk, her sway, her breasts. Or so he thought at first. Before her husband's departure, she was swollen from long, restless, sleepless nights of love. Desperate at the thought that he would not return, she showered him with greedy, shameless kisses. She had grown jealous; she pictured him having an affair with every Friulian or Venetian girl he met. She tried to make their parting so sweet that every day he would think of returning to her.

She tried everything: she put on her best gowns from Trieste and Venice, all delicate lace; she pulled her silk stockings up and tied them around her legs; she fastened her vests tight around her breasts. Then – just as impulsively – she removed them all. Though scarcely in the mood to sing, sing she did, and drink as well, and kissed her husband's neck, chest, lips, ears.

During the weeks he spent with them, Arandjel grew sallow and gaunt; he was in hell. He experienced the great imperial city as a madhouse, a hodgepodge of soldiers, horses, greybeard dandies, half-naked coquettes, and assorted Court officers and artisans running in circles. He made a thousand or so thalers selling silver to a friend, a Greek by the name of Demitrios Kopsha, so he could not be said to be wholly unhappy, but his ennui was beyond words. As a boy he had loved his brother because he was stronger and because he spoke the language of the Gypsies; he loved him as time went on because their late father willed him to and because Vuk was a crazed and reckless soldier who feared only him, Arandjel, his younger brother. Having fleeced him of his entire inheritance at the time of their father's death, Arandjel eventually took pity on him and, as he was growing richer by the day, helped him back to his feet with great brotherly feeling. Now, for the first time, the man seemed an utter stranger to him.

To go to headquarters at Court, which he did every day, Vuk Isakovič put on his best trousers and a powdered wig, trimmed his mustachio, and decked himself out in his medals, his blue ribbons wide as a hand, and his knife thin as a finger. From the time he began delivering messages to the Court for Patriarch Šakabenta and working with Count Geisruch on a census of Slavonian military villages, he had become worried and taciturn, but also haughty. Arandjel was put off by Vuk's new behaviour and lost all brotherly feeling for him; nor did he see why he should feel anything at all for that nose, those yellowish, perpetually bloodshot eyes, for that oversized bumpkin dressed like a scarecrow. He spent his weeks in Vienna utterly aimless, smoking incessantly and frantically telling his beads. The thought that his many-times-wounded, decrepit brother was again leaving for the field aroused no pity in him, nor did the thought that in a matter of weeks he might be all alone in the world, brotherless as well as fatherless. There would be other people, there would be his boats; he would go on trading, eating, telling his beads. His brother meant nothing to him; what did he care about Vuk's gastric disorders, or his dealings with the monks, which he spoke of day and night, or his children, with whom he wished to saddle him? And he told Vuk so.

As for his sister-in-law, she was no longer the marvellous woman with the infant in her arms, the woman he had kissed, trembling with sinful desire, filled with awe and melancholy. He now found her distasteful. In the morning he saw her in bed, still warm and eyes dilated from amorous frolic. At night he heard her cooing to her husband, tempting him early to bed. During the day he would see her in tears, tantrums, or embraces, making her toilet, clinging to her husband's neck. Truth to tell, it was only when she was inflamed by passion, wanton, that she was beautiful, but that was a truth which held

43

for all women. What, then, aroused his spleen? This woman who was more than a little besotted by nightfall? Her tearful, sickly girls? His brother's scars, medals, glory? His brother could fall from his horse and break his neck in Italy for all he cared; he would get precious little sympathy from him. And he told him so.

Vuk returned from Italy, but Arandjel stayed away from him, still harbouring a vague desire for the body of his sister-in-law.

Not until the fourth time Vuk was about to go off to war did Arandjel consent to go and see him. On his way he stopped in Zemun to inspect the house he had bought as a base from which to trade with the Turks. Suspecting nothing, he proceeded to his brother's in the same mood as when he had left him – all malice, envy, and distaste. His brother, who looked older, different, was not happy to see him. At the sight of his sister-in-law, however, Arandjel was thunderstruck.

No longer was she the child bride, or the beautiful young mother with the head of an infant resting on her breast, or the buxom woman he had heard, through the wall, billing and cooing all night. This was a woman he had never seen before.

Her pallor, framed by hair and brows several shades darker, was complete: the glimmer that hovered over her forehead and cheekbones reminded him of white silk Venetian eye masks; only her nostrils were pink. As for her mouth, it was smaller than it had been, paler, with an odd smile that never left it, not even when she looked at him sadly. And when she looked at him with her big round eyes, he felt he was anchoring at the shore of a deep blue sea.

She made believe he was a complete stranger and asked him questions she had never asked before. Oh, if only his brother would die in the war, he would think – and then feel such horror, he would cross himself. She no longer paraded before him; she merely stood straight and tall, ripe and comely, unaware perhaps that he was trembling. She was

44

more beautiful than ever. She often touched him wordlessly, and one evening as she was changing into a new Venetian gown, she left her door open so he could watch.

She lied. He caught her in the act almost immediately. Beautiful and serene even when lying, she had lied to her husband, and with a gleaming white smile. She ruled over the house; she ruled over the fields, which were then being ploughed near the water; she ruled over the livestock, over the servants and shepherds, over the entire village. Everyone hated her and feared her. Feared her smile.

She entrusted the children to her maidservants; only in her husband's presence did she hold them in her lap. With a smile. One morning she asked her brother-in-law whether he did not find that his brother had suddenly aged. On that day Arandjel Isaković offered his Zemun house as a refuge for his brother's wife and children while Vuk was off fighting.

And so Dame Dafina came to stay in the house of her brother-in-law. She was to live there with her daughters for several months, for a year perhaps, until her husband returned from the war; she was also to deliver her third child there, for she was in the family way, in her third month, of which her husband learned only shortly before his departure.

Accompanied by two carriages laden with clothing, she arrived all but unnoticed by the Zemun notables in blue Turkish jackets, black fur hats and boots and Austrian caps and Greek fustanellas, who had gathered to catch a glimpse of her.

Upon settling the children and their servants in a triangular corner in the attic, whose floor sagged perilously under the weight of mouse-infested sacks of flour, she chose for herself a spacious room with numerous rugs, a fine wooden floor and beams, a large clay stove, and, as she noted at once, two doors. Then she set about reorganizing the household. She was particularly drawn to a large barred window that looked out upon

45

the river. It was there she chose to sit and cry her eyes out those first few days. Day and night, broad and stagnant, the river flowed. And in it her shadow.

Even though she maintained daily crying hours, she managed to have half of Zemun call on her: officers' wives, Greek and Austrian matrons, merchants' daughters much younger than she, the wives of her brother-in-law's and husband's friends and all their daughters, a fat Turkish woman with droopy eyelids who had survived the siege of Belgrade, and even a pair of Walachian sisters of whose origins and occupation nothing was known.

Plying them with coffee, sherbet, and nargilehs, she learned what there was to be learned about Zemun, and Zemun learned what she had to tell. Soon she discovered that houses in Zemun were painted either yellow or blue, that some were high, others low; she also learned which house belonged to whom. She learned who had died in the house on the corner and who was vomiting excessively in the house with the large mulberry tree; she learned which merchant wished to marry off his son and which to marry off his daughter, and who they hoped would marry whom. The conversation turned to childbirth. She learned how many women were expecting this month and how many next month, and that a mother of six, who had died after ingesting a concoction of ashes and vinegar to prevent conception, was now seen nightly flying on a white sheet; she learned that Dimče Diamanti had brought home a mistress and that he, she, and his lawfully wedded wife were all living together. There was also talk of how her husband, Major Vuk Isakovič, had been taken in chains from Pécs to the fortress at Temesvár, where he remained until Baron Engelshofen happened to find him and, having embraced him, ordered him released, as a result of which he would soon be returning, with seven men from Zemun, and not go to war at all. And she learned that Nikola Panajot's daughter had come back from Vienna with petticoats that

46

barely reached the knee. And that she, Dafina, was lame in her left leg.

What Zemun learned from her was that boiled sugar mixed with oil makes a good remedy for the vomiting of bile; that in nearby Belgrade there was a midwife, a Turkish midwife, who made a special brandy that women drank once a month in a steaming bath and that eliminated all worry of having children; that the war was now in full swing and that her husband was no longer in Pécs with his men, having sent his brother a letter the previous week from a town called Radkersburg; and that in Venice she had seen more than petticoats barely reaching the knee, she had seen *gowns* that barely reached the knee, though only in front – in back they touched the ground and even dragged along it.

Zemun also learned that she had been an orphan at the time of her marriage to Isakovič and that she thought he would be like a father to her for the first year, until their first child was born, and only then would he become her husband; that she was nearly always alone and therefore spent much time weeping; that Isakovič had had many women, wicked, evil women, Walachian, Hungarian, and Austrian, whereas his brother, Arandjel, who had offered her his house as a refuge, preferred Greek, Armenian, and Venetian women, in whose languages he was conversant; that the wife of the Prince of Württemberg had fallen in love with Isakovič while living in Belgrade, in the mansion where the Pasha now lived; and that she cried every night because of nightmares in which her husband appeared to her as a corpse or in the frightening form of a beast or toad or rat. As for the rumour that she was lame in her left leg, she would gladly exhibit both her legs – front and back – to refute it.

Thus did Dafina Isakovič come to know Zemun and Zemun to know her. She never left the house, and she wept a great deal.

Though her dealings with the world were simple, down-to-earth, natural, her dealings with her brother-in-law were far from such, and might better be described as supernatural. For the most part she kept silent, her eyes moist, her smile mysterious. When she did speak, she spoke of the night, which she feared, and of the darkness, which she perceived as full of apparitions; she spoke of her youth, which had passed, and of life, which she found so burdensome. Eyes overflowing, she spoke of her husband, who no longer seemed to love her and perhaps never had.

She would stand before him, her bosom high, her hands masking the despair in her face. She never raised her voice or reclined on the rugs scattered over the floor when he was present. Nor did she receive women guests. The day was for them; the evening was for him. He did not hear her gossip or giggle. She reserved a different voice for him, a different look; everything about her was different. Nor was she the only one: her servants, too, without actually being told, acted differently in his presence. A hush would come over the house; the candles would be put under glass; everything was made pleasant for him.

Without quite sharing Arandjel Isakovič's conviction that she was a rare beauty, she knew her worth. Her feet, which he compared to those of a robust angel, had never pleased her, and she hid them under her silk robes, showing only the tips of her fine slippers. She was, however, proud of her calves and knees, fully sharing her brother-in-law's assessment and showing them off whenever possible by crossing her legs. She would also parade around him with a vigorous, straight-backed gait, swinging her hips. Her hands, which had not yet touched his neck, twisted and slithered like a snake in its vicinity. She would also press her breasts to him as lovers press cheek to cheek. But most of all she relied on her eyes. She gazed upon him sadly.

Skilled merchant that he was, Arandjel Isakovič understood exactly what was at stake. He understood that the timid orphan this woman had been as a girl, having been forced to accept solitude and unfulfilled desires, was a timid orphan no longer: she had grown into a sound, healthy animal that gave ferocious chase to her bear of a husband. What he could not understand was what she wanted now.

He was impatient. Appalled by the thing he intended to do, he wished to lose no time. He did not wish to think of the consequences; he tried to put his brother out of his mind, but the picture of the massive figure riding in his coach, all silver medals and white plumes, kept rising before his eyes. Tortured by lack of sleep and pangs of conscience, resolved to let no look, no nod, no sigh betray him, he hoped that what he contemplated would take place out of sight, under cover, as in a dream. And, above all, that no one would be hurt. Though consumed by desire and the shameless dreams he had of her every night, he had no wish to start a long relationship; he had no wish to steal her from his brother and live long years with her. He was even mad enough to picture himself informing Vuk about it afterwards, the two of them driving her away, and begging his forgiveness, making peace with him – they were brothers, after all.

In the hope of winning her, he showered her with gifts. He tried suggestive words and deeds to move her to action. She was not moved. She gazed at him serenely with her beautiful, luminous, winter-evening eyes as if stars were shining above them. She took his words full of guile as heartfelt, his scheming blandishments as genuine. In the evening, after a day of inanities, she became wise and discriminating with him.

She caused him such torment – he had grown sallow from hope and anticipation and looked pathetic in his long blue caftan – that he resolved at last to touch her. At first her hands, then her hair. Once, when she had been crying at the bedside of her ailing daughter, he lifted her under the arms and, trembling all over, kissed her.

But all his words and suggestions she turned into concern

for the family, brushing away his hands, pretending not to see the desire behind them, continuing to gaze upon him with her limpid icy-blue eyes. Arandjel was so inflamed that in her very indifference he saw the will to accept the inevitable.

As in his dealings with silver, he tried to measure the degree of her consent, but she would not allow it to be measured. She gave no sign, not the slightest hint. She was immaculate, glacial, absent. It looked as if she would never give herself to him, not in this world at least. The fact was, she simply wanted him to take her by force.

For Dame Dafina, who had grown up among merchants and worshippers of Mammon, understood exactly what was at stake. She was in no hurry. Nor was she eager to give herself to this young, dry, sallow brother-in-law who reminded her of her own brothers. She felt nothing but repugnance for his yellow fingernails, his scraggly black monkish moustache and beard, his pale eyes, thin nose, and yellow teeth always sticky from sweets. She thought of him as an emaciated version of her husband. If, during her conversations with her brother-in-law, she felt a glimmer of desire, it was for her husband. For her huge, massive husband, whom she had once adored and who even now, drained and aging as he was, could look – on horseback, at least – as strong as a bear.

Once so hot-blooded and sensual that she suffered constant migraines, she turned cold in this house, where her husband had left her to wait after tricking her upon his departure and humiliating her in the eyes of the world, and all because he feared the tears, wailing, and fainting that no departure could be without. She had never been exposed to temptation, nor had anyone but her husband approached her. Had anyone dared approach her in the first few years of her marriage, shame and humiliation would have caused her to leap into the stagnant river that flowed beneath her window. Had Arandjel dared to do so the previous year, she would have pacified him with her tears, her prayers, her sisterly kisses; she would have made him see the light, distracted him from his purpose, dissuaded him from sending her soul, along with his, straight to perdition.

But now she had no qualms about feeling his breath on her, seeing his shadow on her in the semidarkness of early evening when he pretended to have something to tell her. She felt much as she felt when she watched her shadow in the restless water flowing day and night beneath her window. She was alone and uncertain her husband would return. He had gone off, far away, with his wild men, his horses and dogs and his potbelly.

She wanted to see what her brother-in-law would do if he went completely mad one day; she wanted it to happen if only to relieve the boredom, the bottomless pit in which she sometimes felt herself suspended headfirst. And recalling how in her desire she would bend convulsively over her husband, kissing his chest, neck, and ears, she wondered how his brother would kiss, bent over her arms, her legs, her lap. She sensed his fear and indecision, yet realized that it would take less than nothing to hurl them with a howl into the river's murky depths. Smiling, though moved more by horror than desire, she felt the day approaching. After all, she had spent three weeks in his house.

One day the mild spring of blossoming fruit trees was hit by frost and freezing rain, a common occurrence in that part of the world. The wind, battering torrents of rain along the river, caused Arandjel Isakovič's boat, loaded with horses and crossing over to the Turkish side, to fill with water and capsize. Half numb, Arandjel barely escaped with his life.

They carried him home. He arrived amid such a din of wailing and lamentation that no one raised an eyebrow when Dafina, scarcely moving her blue lips, ordered him to be placed in her room on the large stove next to the wide Venetian bed. She was terrified that he might die and leave her and her children unprotected, a prey to his Gypsy servants, all brigands as far as she was concerned.

Isakovič and his men had spent that morning crossing a narrow footbridge near the town of Kremsmünster in Austria. The troops were in disarray.

A hare ran across his path.

I only hope that the bridge holds, he thought, and that my belongings do not fall into the river. Then, staring up at the cloudless sky, he reined in his horse and asked the captain riding beside him, "What means this sign at noon, Piščević? We have come this far safe and sound, but now the wind stirs the dust like a curtain. Could it be that my first-born daughter is doing battle with an illness?"

It never occurred to him that at that very moment his wife might be deceiving him.

4

Vuk Isakovič Has Departed,
but All Fruska Gora Has Followed Him

Arandjel Isakovič floundered in the cold water next to a horse churning the mire with its front legs and roiling the water with its hind ones. When the boat capsized, the ramparts of Belgrade capsized too, or so it seemed to him, and for a moment all he could see was sky. But the next moment the river was rushing past his eyes, an immensely broad river, broader than it had ever appeared from the boat or the shore, which now looked impossibly far, a journey of two or three hours. Then he sank headlong into a yellow-green bottomless mass, which turned dark and icy as it closed over him.

Surfacing again, among horses wild with fright, he was unable to call for help; his throat was clogged with sand. The water beneath him was so turbulent that he feared being dragged down feet first, then arms, then head, into an abyss from which he could neither climb nor crawl. His fingers – the nails crammed with horsehair, which even filled his mouth – finally managed to grab hold of some reeds, a tree stump. Only then was he pulled out, slime dripping from his eyes, ears, and nose.

As they carried him home, he thought triumphantly, shivering deliriously, of his head emerging from the jumble of croups, hooves, and muzzles, but then he thought more often of himself with arms flailing, as if sinking, drowning in the terrifying chaos of horseflesh, debris, and icy waves.

53

After stripping him, rubbing him down with sand, and wrapping him in sheepskins, they carried him to his house like a corpse, though his eyes were wide open. Blue and shivering, he felt weightless, as if his body were made of birds on the verge of flight. Lying there on a rug, he was afraid to move, for the banks of the river, the reeds, the sky, even his house seemed on the point of dissolving, flowing away.

As they carried him through the weeping and wailing and the beating of wings, through the mud, over the planks, he suddenly felt a mad desire to be carried into her room. His tradesman's instinct told him the time had come to purchase her.

Reclining on the clay stove beside her bed, he felt he had ascended to heaven. His brother never crossed his mind, nor did his brother's children. He was off by himself, in a pleasant deep shade, and had no need to bring his brother into it; he was on his own and he would win the woman. Safe from the water and mire, redolent of the *rakija* they had kneaded into his body, he hovered luxuriantly in the heat that radiated from the large stove. With the ceiling above, his sister-in-law's white bed below, and the yellow walls all around, he felt completely cut off from the world. Here, in his own home, he felt utterly secure. No one would know. She would not talk; he was certain of it. It would all be like a dream. Within these four walls they could do as they pleased; they were as elusive and free as their shadows. Outside the wind was howling. Inside, it was warm. The fire crackled.

Burning from the heat, he was nevertheless fully conscious of what he was about to undertake. He ordered the servants to change his clothes once more. She moved over to the window for the sake of propriety, averting her eyes, yet she did not leave the room. Nor did she leave after they had placed him in her bed. He, meanwhile, continued to luxuriate, his limbs still partially numb, feeling her close to him in the dim warmth of the fire. No one would disturb them now; it was an opportunity not to be missed.

54

The flames in the stove lit the large room, turning everything in it to giant shadows. Though possessed of all his faculties, safe and sound, washed and dressed, Arandjel had a leaden look. He lay in the white bed as if he were about to give up the ghost. Towering shadows of the bed, table, and a black chest fell on the hot wall like the shadows of trees in summer. In the perfect silence of the semidarkness, Dafina pressed her face to the bars on the window and listened to the water flowing endlessly below.

His eyes shut tight, Arandjel could hear the house making ready for bed. Lest the servants be summoned, he made no requests; he moved as little as possible under his red quilt, which almost totally hid him and whose undulations he saw as a boundless sea, though his heartbeat resonated like a hammer in his brain. Immobile, his eyes almost shut, he waited for the fire to burn down, for the darkness.

Dafina, who sat in a high chair that showed off her sturdy legs, orange stockings, and gold slippers to good advantage, was still leaning against the windowsill. She wore a white gown made of numerous pieces of silk which, sewn together, resembled acacia blossoms and draped loosely over her shapely belly. Her head was bowed, the ends of her mouth turned upward in a smile. Though petrified at the thought that her brother-in-law intended to spend the night in her bed, she had dismissed her maid. Now she wound a towel doused in vinegar around his head and placed a small icon of Saint Mrata on his chest, under his shirt, tickling him accidentally, unbearably, with her long fingers.

For the hundredth time Arandjel Isakovič reassured himself that no one would ever know. She would not talk, he was certain, and because for years in his dreams he had licked her hands like an obedient dog, he now burned with the desire to crush her, bite her, tear her limb from limb. Not that he thought it would happen from one moment to the next. Not after so lengthy a period of bargaining. But for the first time he felt confident rather than intimidated. Within these four yellow walls nothing he feared on the outside existed; the outside ceased to exist. Within these four yellow walls he could do as he pleased. It seemed perfectly absurd that she should be his brother's wife when his brother was absent, and even more absurd that she could not be his wife as well; it seemed perfectly absurd that someone might intervene and ask questions. Although he still trembled at the thought of the scandal that would ensue were someone to catch them in the act, he was reassured by the silent semidarkness and the four yellow walls.

Outside, the wind howled, the dogs barked, the water flowed, its unbroken murmur filtering up to the room through the windows. Yet the room was quiet enough to hear the mice racing behind the shadows on the wall.

The fortress of Belgrade, the colourful Turkish bazaar, the drowning horses, his large blue house, the mud, the nets, the boats, the eddies, the whitewashed stove – they all swirled around in his head, only to vanish in the warm dark silence of the room the moment his eyes lit on her, sitting at the window. He could hardly breathe from the effort of finding the words that would bring her to the bed.

He could feel her approach. His brother, who for three weeks had been no more to him than a distant heap of uniforms, epaulettes, greatcoats, and plumes, had completely ceased to exist. He pictured him – tried to picture him – beside this woman, but in vain: he was not here. Even his brother's daughters, whom he knew to be asleep just above him, whom he had heard wake up in the middle of the night and cry for their mother, had ceased to exist: they were invisible.

The woman sitting at the window belonged to him; he was certain of it. She would lie at his side, kissing him, murmuring his name, cooing. She might be burning with desire for another, but she could not have that other. Like the wind, like the water beneath the window, Vuk could not return. And not even his servant Ananije, who always slept at his door, could enter this room. Her husband was far away, her stepfather, the beardless Christodoulos, who still owed Arandjel for a delivery of tobacco, was far away, and neither his partner, Dimče Diamanti, nor the priest would sway him, not with all their inane arguments. Everything outside these walls would stay outside, and she would stay here, here, at his side. No one would know. He was certain she would not talk.

He felt a sudden drunken joy. Water, reeds, sand, sky – they were all far away. Zemun, too, which insisted on knowing everything, and her husband, who might never return. But she was here, with him.

He raised his hand, and a large black shadow appeared on the wall. To beckon her silently to bed. To undress. Why should she drowse, fully dressed, by the window? He would lie on the floor and she on the bed, still dressed, if it calmed her fear. Or he would extinguish the light while she undressed and lie down next to her only after she had fallen asleep. If it calmed her fear.

But just as he was about to speak, she tumbled off her chair with a bloodcurdling scream, her hands trembling, her face white as chalk, wide-eyed, open-mouthed, incapable of speech. Exhausted from her vigil, frightened and distracted, she had been on the point of drifting off to sleep when her husband appeared to her, walking on the water beneath the window, unclad, unkempt, drenched in blood, and carrying an enormous club that reached to the ceiling.

She was awakened by the sound of her brother-in-law opening the door. He stood in the doorway, his blue caftan, yellowish face, flat nose, wispy beard, and thinning hair framed, like a continuation of her dream, in the pale light of morning. For a moment she saw a corner of the roof and a single branch; then the narrow band of light on the wall shrank to nothing, and the room was dark again.

Naked and covered with sweat, she nearly screamed. All she could see in the dark, after pushing her hair from her eyes, was the white of the stove and the window curtain and the black of the large chest in which she kept her clothes; all she could hear was the unbroken murmur of the water below the window. Clutching her knees, then digging her hands into her tangled hair, she tried to understand what had happened.

She had spent the night with her brother-in-law.

At first she refused to believe it. She felt nothing, she was not tired or sleepy; she had had her usual good night's rest – alone, she assumed at first, waking. But as she stretched, she discovered traces of a night of love and was disgusted. Suddenly, full of hate, she sensed him there in the darkness, lying at her side – his hands, his teeth, his beard; she heard him laugh and felt her arms fly out for his scrawny neck.

She sat bolt upright and covered her face with her hands. Yet through her fingers, through the darkness, in her mind's eye, she saw all the loathsome, monstrous things he had done to her. She could almost feel him licking her hands and knees again. It was as if a dog had jumped on to the bed. Terrified, she pulled the quilt up over her, bumping her head against the stove. Now fully aware of what she had done, she wanted to scream. Arandjel had looked so unspeakably foul, weak, ridiculous that night.

Instead, she burst into tears, and with such vehemence that she all but took pleasure in them. Had her husband come to comfort her, she would have told him why she did it: she would have told him she did it because he had publicly disgraced her on the day of his departure by failing to take proper leave of her; she would have told him she did it because he constantly left her, went off alone, moved from place to place like a Gypsy. And because she needed a refuge from the eternal swamps and marshes and bogs.

She saw the day dawn: light crept in under the door, objects emerged from the darkness, the bars on the window appeared slowly behind the curtain. She turned on to her back and continued to weep, the tears flowing down her cheeks. She was so full of sorrow that she failed to hear the animals bleating and braying in the mud below the house, which put her out of sorts every morning, or to notice that the fire in the stove had gone out. She had often wept over her fate since her husband began going to seed; her life when she was a young girl seemed utter misery to her, the life of a servant. And living with a husband who constantly left her was like living in a pit from which she hopelessly tried to escape.

Weeping even more bitterly, she conjured up her husband's face and, burying her head in the pillow, started kissing that face. Vuk Isakovič had been a handsome man when he married her: his cool, smooth skin was a source of endless pleasure to her; his yellowish eyes speckled with black had not lost their radiance, and she never forgot their glint beneath his long, thick lashes, just as one never forgets a golden rain at sunset at the edge of a young forest. Nor could she forget his soft, silky hair, now greying, or his pink upper lip, which quivered when he laughed. She had heard it said that he beat his men and horses on the head with his fists and leaped over tables when drunk; she had heard all the terrible gossip about his women, Walachian and Hungarian. But the Vuk she knew was different. From the start he lived a secret life with her.

For nearly two years after their sudden, loveless marriage he acted like a courteous stranger, kissing her gently, cautiously, as if to make sure not to shatter her, tall, beautiful, fragile as she was. After coming home late in the evening, sweaty and dirty, from a day of jumping ditches with his young officers or teaching recruits to hurl barrels of gunpowder into a trench, he would take her riding, sometimes all night, through fields and woods, up hills under the stars.

Unable to converse with her during their first few months together – for she did not know German, and he knew neither Greek nor Venetian – he made do with songs and dances, glances and kisses. As he rarely had the opportunity to take her to balls in Brod or at the Osijek fortress, they made do with fox hunts, which for months on end were his only diversion. And so it was with the soft, moist earth and grass, the bushes burgeoning in April, the fragrant green hillsides and clear vernal skies that the young wife first inhaled the aroma of her husband. She was as if bewitched. No worldly treasure, no whip or serpent would have made her renounce that man and his curious smile, the likes of which she had never seen, not on her stepfather's face or on her brothers' or on the face of any Greek.

Whether leaning against a luxuriant tree at the crest of a hill or lolling beneath it, on his back, exhausted from lovemaking, he always appeared to her pure of countenance, untouched by the vicissitudes of life that Arandjel Isakovič described to her. All she had to do was recall the early years of her marriage, and rolling hills, budding branches, sweeping Slavonian valleys, and rollicking clouds arose before her eyes. Nights full of wild grass, forest darkness, underbrush with red fruit, the gurgle of streams, and, most of all, the bright sky, the stars – such were the memories of her first years with Vuk Isakovič. Now, through her tears, she pictured him and his skin, eyes, and lips as plants and constellations. But suddenly his current image took over, and he was once more a bowlegged, bloated man, heavy as a barrel.

She stopped crying. A shudder passed through her at the thought of how fast those beautiful years had flown: he had gone off to war, she had had her first child. He returned from the war stout and crotchety. No more balls at the fortress, fewer fox hunts. He and his father had settled a village outside the town of Varadin, and that spring he led the men out to plough, tramping barefoot through marshes, knee-deep in mud. In the interminable boredom of the year in which she nursed her firstborn, she felt that he had come to look upon her, with his glittering yellow eyes, as a household object, like the bed or the stove or the chest where she kept her dresses. His father was to blame. His father took him everywhere with him.

When he left the army, ostensibly for reasons of health, and entered trade, she lost all her zest for life. He constantly left her alone, on a boat anywhere between Galatz and Vienna, with little or no money; nor did he ask any questions upon his return. After he rejoined the army, their life was gay again for a while, but then he went off on his second campaign. Moreover, he had begun to frequent the local monks, and changed greatly under their influence. He returned taciturn, altogether withdrawn, and fat.

By the time he went off on his third campaign, she no longer tried to hold him back. If she still showered him with kisses, the passion was feigned, the tears far from bitter. Nor did his eyes sparkle any longer. Yet kiss him she did, like any jealous but robust young wife trying to make the most of the last moments and therefore turning a blind eye to reality. She felt deep down that he no longer loved her, that he would not return alive. When he did return, he was transformed, strange, gone to seed. He built a church in the middle of the village. He looked more like her father now than her husband.

Yet there was still a bond between them, a bond of veiled sensuality. Strange and melancholic as he was, he looked at her in a way he looked at no other being. And the pleasure he gave her was unlike any other. His face, his voice, his name, his touch, the mere thought of him still had the power to stir her. All else was an endless plain of muddy snow.

Thus did Dame Dafina – weary from tears, nodding off again – remember her husband. Shivering from the chill that kept insinuating its way into her bed, she opened her still-moist eyes at last and saw that it had long been day – rainy, dreary, and cold.

*

Like all women, Dafina Isakovič had known days of sadness and grief, but not one was so sad and bleak as this, the first day after her adultery.

She had at other times pondered on how pitiful a creature a woman was – a toy, an appliance – and thought of her life as a complete void. But never had God's treatment of His creatures seemed so repulsive as on that day, in the house of her brother-in-law. Her father's house, all merchandise, tobacco, and cloth; her aunt's room, with its icons and lamps, where they had asked for her hand; and the many houses and rooms she had lived in with her husband – they all passed through her memory. Sad and empty, meaningless, yet they seemed almost pleasant by comparison with the four yellow walls, the din of the river, the shadows of the bed and stove, all so terrifying in their constancy, rigidity, inertia.

Yet she felt no remorse – what good was remorse? – when she thought of what she had done. Nor did she give much thought to how she might keep it secret. She did not particularly care whether her husband found out about it, wherever he was, out there in the world. The only thing that grieved her was the prospect of having another child.

For had he not willed the infidelity? Had he not gone off time after time, leaving her, as he left his horses and servants, with no mercy, no compassion, no reason? He would go off to war, a harrowing enterprise and totally alien to her; why, the mere thought of his sabre scar was enough to make her gorge rise. What did his wife mean to him anyway? Was he not more concerned with his church, his men, and his horses than with her? And did he include her in the love he felt for his children? And how many women had he had on the side?

The more she thought, the more relieved she felt. At least the new man would maintain her in luxury, in style; he would not move her from place to place. No, she did not expect her husband to return. This time he would not return. He would appear in her memory now and then on a hill or in a wood; he would appear in her dreams, handsome as a stag at twilight. Yet there would be days when she found his image repulsive, like a bear in a fetid cave. And again she burst into tears. If that was what love was, she would live without it, she would live with this dry, sallow man who weighed out silver on his scales and licked her hands submissively like a dog. Her life would be peaceful, lovely, free from the clamour, the uproar, the chaos her husband brought with him each time he returned.

Now Arandjel no longer seemed so repugnant to her. Indeed, recalling certain details of the previous night, she smiled a distinctly prurient smile. Sensations she had not known with her husband now struck her as more exciting than they had the night before. Her brother-in-law was perhaps more of a match for her than she had imagined. Perhaps he was the natural successor to her first, ruthless and violent, husband, and although she could not say she cared for him as much, she had to admit he had courted her with great skill. She decided that instead of scolding him she would make him ask for her hand.

When her servants came, she began to fret and quake once more at the thought of what she had done, but their placid faces calmed her. They had left their wooden slippers at the door as usual and approached her without a word. She was silent for a while, and even covered her eyes with her hands. At last she said she would remain in bed all day because she had a headache. When they told her that Arandjel Isakovič had gone to Belgrade to deliver to some Turkish customers the horses among which he had nearly drowned, a slight shudder ran through her, and she asked them to bring water for her bath.

And so the day passed in trifles, Dafina in no way showing what she had been through. However, it was obvious that she had been crying, which fact soon made the rounds of the house servants. Then old Ananije, who slept at her door with a large rusty scimitar for a pillow, reported that he had heard

63

her shriek at one point. Before long it was rumoured that Vuk Isakovič had appeared to his wife and his brother dripping with blood and carrying his head, either riding a gigantic toad or walking on the water. That was why the dogs had howled so, the servants concluded. Besides, had not the late Lazar Isakovič, brandishing his sword like an arms merchant, appeared to them eight years before? And all because his son failed to pierce his heart with a needle when he died.

The first day of adultery seemed indeed insignificant to Dafina. By nightfall all she felt was that something unusual was yet to happen.

The morning had passed in tears, thought, and preening, the afternoon in waiting for Arandjel's return from Belgrade; but the afternoon in the large yellow house, so stuffed with flour it might have been a mill, flowed on and on, like the unbroken stream of water beneath the window. Dafina felt like screaming. Anything to break the silence. It was as suffocating as the stale smell of wheat and rye.

Although she felt no remorse at having deceived her husband, she was sick at the thought that it had changed nothing. She had spent the night with her brother-in-law, yet not a single grain of oats in the attic above their heads had moved an inch as a result. She used to feel that for all her power she lay about the house like an object, ignored; now she wanted the house to revolve around her. She was irritated by dead, inert things, things always the same. She wanted her brother-in-law to promise to marry her and take her away, to the new house in Buda.

She had the servants bring in her daughters, but that was no help. The younger girl, all scabs, simply lay there, wound in swaddling clothes like an infant, sucking her thumb, wriggling her feet, staring up at the ceiling with her black-speckled yellowish eyes, unaware that she had been moved from one room to another. The elder girl timorously yet joyfully rushed to her mother's lap, only to rush off again immediately to play hide-and-seek amid the brightly coloured dresses hanging behind the stove. Before long Dafina had nothing to say to the girls, no desire to minister to them: they looked so feeble-minded, so alien. Nor did they show any interest in her; they were more attracted to the bars on the window and especially the fire in the stove. Even when in her arms, they screamed and reached for objects out of their reach, as if struggling to escape from a wicked giant. Finally she dismissed them, along with the servants and the dogs.

She had Dimče Diamanti's wife sent for – the lawful one – a long, dark broomstick of a woman behind a plethora of veils who spent all day dusting furniture yet knew how to read cards and liked to talk, always fingering a certain wart as she did so. She was of no help either. All Franka Diamanti could tell Dafina was that one of the horses that nearly drowned had attacked her husband, who had raced down to the riverbank to help the victims, especially his partner, Arandjel Isakovič, and all of Zemun was talking about it. Then she left.

And so, as night began to fall, Dame Dafina was alone again, alone and deeply depressed by the wet, dreary day from which she had expected so much.

It all seemed so senseless: what she had done – and what she had not done. Everything her brother-in-law had said during the past weeks was right. But clearly as she pictured her night of love with him, she felt that she could not let it go and never think of it again, especially if her husband were to return home unexpectedly. She also felt that adultery would bring her little happiness. She could commit adultery again, with someone new, the next day, and think nothing of it. She would do better to think of the comforts and wealth that would be hers if she married her brother-in-law. She pictured the new dresses she would order, feeling the silk slide over her body as if she already owned them. But she derived no satisfaction from her fantasies, she felt all the sadder for them:

it seemed to make no difference whether she belonged to one brother or the other, or to both – or yet to another, as she now realized, any other.

She stared out of the window at the vast twilight, the cold, grey mist above the water, the river turbid and yellow, swollen with mud, the willows all buds yet coated with hoarfrost by the sudden cold spell. Above the islands, deep in the moist evening sky, she beheld the vast luminous blue pierced by the minarets and ramparts of Belgrade. The croaking of frogs rose on all sides.

A broad swatch of sky threw light on one wall of the room, where Dafina all but writhed in lethargy and despair on her bed, having abandoned one of her gold brocade slippers behind the stove and the other at the door. She thought of extinguishing the lamp beneath a large old icon of Christ, but fear of the impending darkness overcame her. She remained on her back, on the cushions, scarcely moving, in the cloud of her own tobacco smoke. Her head was so heavy, she barely noticed the room sinking into night. Soon only the grey evening light glancing off the river was left, and it was lost between the curtains and the bed, so that the large dark chest in which she stored her dresses rose black from the floor like a stately gravestone.

Through the smoke of Turkish cigarettes she sought the light of the window as one seeks the light of the moon through the dark of night. All at once she heard the scurry of mice behind her. She wanted to scream, but the scream stuck in her throat. Except for the white stove, on which like a ghost a sheet hung drying, and the bright gash of the window, the room was plunged in darkness. Table, door, bed – they were all invisible; even the slippers on the rug beside her. Outside, the dogs had begun to howl.

Smothered by darkness, she could not scream; overwhelmed by fear, she could not stir. She felt a sudden chill in her feet, and soon her whole body was shivering. Yet she could not bring herself to move; indeed, the more she tried to prop herself up, the deeper she dug into the cushions.

She saw the sheet rise from the stove. She saw the black chest open wide and a swarm of mice stream forth. With the scream still stuck in her throat, her eyes bulging, she saw a ball of toads, serpents, and snails splashing and mashing one another in a pool of mud at the base of the chest. Then the sheet moved in her direction. At the same moment she sensed a presence behind the curtain, a cold breath. Shivering, trying to push her hair from her eyes, she saw a hand emerge from the dark.

One by one the fingers, white as snow, crept closer. The hand descended the wall and crawled over the furniture like a white cat. Suddenly she spied another hand grabbing hold of the dresses behind the stove and flinging them, crumpled, to the floor. As she uttered a muffled scream, she saw a paunch appear in front of the curtain, the enormous paunch of her husband, and then his mouth, eyes, nose, his entire head on the curtain, dripping blood, throat gashed, his black tricorn hovering above it. The wall behind the apparition began to sway, and a field of golden grain entered the room, a stream of oats, wheat, and rye poured down from the attic, while a maelstrom of stars, blue, violet, and yellow, glittered before her eyes, and a strange tepid sea washed over her. She leaped to her feet with a shriek and found herself face to face with a terrifying Vuk Isakovič, by now in an advanced state of decomposition. It was like running into a bear while fleeing a pack of wolves. Trembling, she plunged back into the darkness, on this first day of her adultery, and hurt the child she was carrying inside her.

Thus, with her vapours and fears, with the nocturnal visions of her feverish brain, did Dame Dafina put an end to the peace in Arandjel Isakovič's house during that spring of unusually late frosts and sudden, wanton heat.

*

Dafina was found lying unconscious in the darkness, in a pool of blood. The blood continued to pour from her for two weeks; no midwife was able to stop the flow. Hunched over, skin and bones, sallow, she could scarcely take the four steps from the bed to the barred window, where pillows awaited her and where from morning till night she could watch the water flowing, the islands blossoming, and the sky changing.

Every morning she was seen by an old Turkish healer whom Arandjel Isakovič had brought from Belgrade in his own boat, and who prescribed herb potions to be drunk in a warm bath. Every Wednesday evening she was seen by a physician who came all the way from Osijek, received a ducat a visit, and treated her with metal tubes for an hour, laying her virtually upside down. Otherwise she was free, everyone left her in peace; that is, everyone ignored her: the servants because they feared her, the neighbours because her yellow complexion gave her the look of death, and Arandjel Isakovič – Arandjel Isakovič because he was sickened.

She was a meek, undemanding patient. All that remained of the awful night was the terror in her large, bulging blue eyes. Everything about her had changed. She was dried up, old before her years. She would sit all but motionless at her window, clutching a handkerchief of Venetian lace. The piercing screams she had uttered on that night had given way to silence.

The transformation was so rapid and dire that it affected her brain. The riches and luxury of Buda, her brother-in-law's docile affection, the youth she so longed to enjoy – all had flowed away with her blood. She knew that her beauty had faded, that she would soon be a shadow; she was not surprised when the servants took to neglecting her, and her brother-in-law to avoiding the house. She maintained her silence and spent her days at the window overlooking the water.

There, apart from the rare brightly coloured boat plying its way upstream or down, nothing changed, nor did she hear anything but the deep, hoarse voice of a foghorn. The swallows were late that year; they swooped close to the water and flipped over deftly.

Every day, from the same spot, she saw a swarm of insects as shiny as wind-stirred sand; she saw stakes for the fishermen's nets sticking up from the mud, willows growing darker and thicker overnight, green islands and swaying reeds, and above, in the distance, the fortress on the hill. She grew familiar with the broad expanse of water and the minarets hovering in the warm noon air. She was able to distinguish minute changes in things both visible and invisible. Within a few days she could tell time by the colour of the water and willows; she could predict the weather by the colour of the sky and clouds. She watched a sandbar emerge near one of the islands and the birds come and settle it, especially storks with long red legs. She sensed precisely when the sun would set and what would precede its rise. Sometimes, plagued by insomnia, she took up her place by the window shortly after midnight, to the consternation of the servants, who no longer dared leave her alone at night.

Much as she disdained the person she had become, she never thought of death as imminent or of the hours spent at the window as a gradual dying. Passing her hand through the bars into the mild air, she felt she could almost touch the lukewarm surface of the river flowing past, feel the sand and reeds of the islands, the branches of the willows, now fully in bloom, the warmth radiating from the hilltops, and in the evening, as she undressed for bed, the great endless blue of the sky filled with stars and constellations making their way past the rectangle of her window, pausing there, glittering. Without ever putting it into words, she firmly believed that the doctors would save her life and that, despite the gaping wound in the centre of her body, she would regain her health if not her beauty. After much crying and pleading, she made Arandjel promise to go see Patriarch Šakabenta and find a way to dissolve her marriage to Vuk Isakovič and unite her with him.

She did not tend to the girls; she did not even ask to see them. Her only thought was that they were girls and that as women they would suffer as she had. Her main emotions, as she sat more or less paralysed at the window all those days, were boundless envy of the two men she loved and hated, and endless scorn for herself.

Penury, solitude, affliction – these were a woman's lot, these and staying behind, waiting. She recalled the family house in Trieste, where she had been a brightly dressed doll, or else a servant helping her brothers and doddering stepfather on and off with their clothes morning and night, and scrubbing the scale pans, stone benches, and counter every Saturday. She recalled the early days of her marriage, when she had been happy. She had had children without knowing why, had moved without knowing where, and her joys and sorrows proceeded neither from her reason nor according to her will. So it was with her infidelity, her secret liaison with another man: it had come about according to their will, not hers, inevitably. She was an object, a mere object, and her daughters would be objects too, objects of taking and leaving, kissing and running, licking and beating – all of it completely senseless, pointless. The love the two men had for her, was it not little more than diversion?

Still, had Vuk Isakovič been present, she would not have displeased him. The warmth of spring and of the water would have reminded him of her youth. Pale, ugly, and wrinkled as she was, he would still have found her beautiful. He would have carried her from the bed to the window in his arms. He loved the children and would kiss the children. He would find the perfect spot for her, under the eaves yet in the sun. And she would close her eyes and see the woods brushed with silver moonbeams, the snow-covered fields beyond the Osijek fortress, the fox tracks, the horses and their breath; she would see the past. And he would never leave her again. He would rest his broad hand on her stomach, and the pain would pass.

Even as she wept, Dafina sensed that although she had spent only one night with the other brother – a night so awful, so repulsive, as repulsive as his smooth hands, hard as amber and so timid at first, in the dark – her sympathy now lay more with him. Vuk was gone, and with him the images of their life together, images by now as hazy as the hills she had last seen while taking leave of him.

Arandjel was all she had left, and repulsive as his hands were – the hands to which she had given herself out of something akin to boredom – she caught herself thinking more about them with each day. Yet she was not unaware of the futility of it all. She had entered his house as an object, and as an object she would leave it; she would leave it to make way for another, whom he would flatter with sweet words, shower with silver coins, whose favours he would solicit abjectly, whose body he would cover with passionate kisses. She therefore wished at least to be married, and that as soon as possible.

As for Arandjel Isakovič, he thought he would lose his mind.

No one predicted it for him, nor did he himself foresee it, but the entire house of cards, so carefully constructed, had come down on his head. The bestial lust haunting his dreams, haunting his life all those years, had led him to see the outcome of his love for his sister-in-law in completely different terms; the desire he had tried to stifle all those years had led him to believe that the outcome of his illness would be pleasant, or at least far from unpleasant. And if at times he thought that he could exorcise his sinful passion after a few nights with her, or if at other times he went so far as to think that when the time came he could discard her, as he had discarded any number of servant girls, he knew deep down that he had something else in mind, that what he actually hoped for in his sister-in-law was a haven of long, very long duration.

Having moved so often during his father's lifetime and

71

having experienced so much pain with his wild brother, Arandjel had come to look upon family life, the life of the whole Isakovič tribe – indeed, of the whole population that had migrated with them from Serbia and then back to Serbia – as pure madness. Nothing but mud and marshes in all directions, and men building dugouts to survive the winter, then moving on in spring. He felt a strong desire to put an end to the madness once and for all, to settle down and make the rest of the family follow suit.

Constant quarrels with his father, who had tagged after the Austrian armies, and with his brother, who was now rising rapidly through the ranks, led him to hate them and all those who migrated with them. But plying his trade on colourful boats along the even more colourful Danube ports, he gradually learned to scorn rather than hate. Changes in the landscape, the houses, faces, and people he came in contact with made him self-confident, even arrogant, because, for all his sallow complexion and scaly hands, for all his weakness, *he* did not change, he remained what he was. He derived his strength, a supernatural strength, from his thalers, for he had only to shake them out of his pouch for boats and houses to become his property; indeed, they followed his wishes and desires so perfectly that he came to believe he could make the rain fall and the sun shine for him.

He had conceived a particular hatred for soldiers, who at the command of those senile fops known as officers went off to fight Turks, Frenchmen, Prussians, and Hungarians, and he was ready to curse anyone who wished to go off anywhere. When his brother and some friends began to talk of migrating to Russia, he was the first to denounce them to the military authorities. He also made false accusations against them to the bishops.

What Arandjel really wanted was to unite these people, by now used to a Gypsylike existence, through commerce. He lent money only to those tradesmen and artisans who settled north of the Danube for good, that is, who maintained no illusions about returning to Turkish-occupied Serbia, or for that matter moving to Russia; he used his thalers to sow dissent within the ranks of his family, forcing them to make permanent homes in river towns he chose for them. Travelling the river with herds of livestock to sell and sacks of silver to lend, he always kept an eye out for real estate. In his purchases he gave preference to houses near a church, but also accumulated sties, gardens, and inns as collateral for loans. He had recently bought a house in Pressburg and another in Buda – the latter a huge stone mansion on a hill by the river, with a cellar and storerooms. No, he had no use whatever for talk of going back to Turkey, and still less of migrating to Russia.

His desire for stability and permanence had for years been one with his desire for the body of his sister-in-law, the object of his dreams and of his love, despite the many women proffered him for the night or for a day or two in the course of his travels. Over the years that body had lain at the very core of his life, as if at the bottom of the river he travelled; it had lain there like a rock, impeding his barges, his thoughts, his transactions. It was a magnificent white body, one he hoped would be a haven to him, a haven of long duration.

And God had given it to him.

But now it seemed ready to go back to Vuk Isakovič, to leave him, leave him with only the terrifying bloodstained flux that had flowed ceaselessly for a fortnight into his brain.

5

Departures and Migrations Made Them
as Dim and Fleeting as Smoke After a Battle

While Dame Dafina was falling into the clutches of her brother-in-law, Vuk Isakovič and his men had begun the climb into Styria. After the review at Pécs the men of the Slavonian-Danubian Regiment marched off to war humiliated and mute, like a pack of beaten dogs, and like a herd of cattle they raised dust in two crooked, straggly lines, trampling grass, sand, and mud, skirting villages and marshes. Bivouacking in the long, dark shadows of woods, they woke shivering, as if drunk, their hair and moustaches coated with hoarfrost. They immediately intoned their long-drawn-out Hey... Hey... only to fall silent again as they shouldered their arms and packs and recalled that they knew neither where they were nor where they were bound. They had come to the end of the land they knew from what people in their villages had told them. All they knew about the land beyond was that many of them would not return from it alive.

Their ranks ever closer, their heads ever lower, they moved on like a flock of sheep, passing meadows, passing villages, without seeing them. Every time they crossed a bridge, they crowded and pushed one another brutishly, to no purpose. After several days at a brisk pace the long copper- or silver-studded rifles that doubled as cudgels had chafed away the skin of their right shoulders, and because the pistols, knives, and cartridge pouches strapped around their waists kept

74

sagging, the whole regiment marched with legs spread wide, as if knotty stumps had been tied to the seat of their trousers. Dust, sweat, and tiny black flies stuck to their nostrils and eyelids. Sand grated between their teeth.

The singers marched at the head of the regiment in silence; the officers rode out in front, puffing on their pipes. A pack of mongrels gave chase to the officers' hounds, which, losing their way, would straggle back, through the soldiers, tails between their legs, tongues hanging. Even at a distance the entire regiment stank of tallow.

After several days the men were exhausted, but they pushed on out of inertia. Having ceased to look about them, they took to looking upward, as if hoping to leave the earth. They were overcome by fear of the unknown.

Stopping near strange villages, jostling across unfamiliar bridges, sleeping near wells they could not see in the dark, they began to wonder how they could have been so mad as to set off in the first place. While still in the vicinity of Pécs, they had received bread from relatives in the local villages. Several women had followed their brothers for a full fortnight before turning back. Only now that they went to bed hungry and woke shivering despite the smouldering hayricks did the men realize what they had done: they had left their villages, left everything they knew and understood, to enter a world of which they knew nothing. The peasants they saw in the fields here did their ploughing on horseback. Only the sheep reminded them of their own sheep and home – the sheep and a bay horse or two.

Before long it became clear to everyone that they would not be fighting the Turks, and therefore the country they were crossing seemed all the more mysterious. They were overcome by deep misery.

What they had left behind at home began to dissolve in their memory – and in Vuk Isakovič's, for that matter – like so much smoke. As the hills around them grew into mountains, the marsxy plains and the wells and sties they had started from seemed more and more like a dream, and the images of their wives and children blurred like the mist on the fields they marched past.

But when the trees started changing – first on the horizon, then all around them – when the earth under their feet changed and the air grew thin and crisp, then the men truly lost heart. The changes were too great for them: a river lined with thick woods overrun with boars digging in the moist soil of the underbrush; hawks circling overhead, following them to foothills they had to climb.

The men felt the same void as their commander: they had forgotten their homesteads, put their wives and children out of their heads, and were increasingly occupied with the daily misery and sweat. But they were tormented more by the pain within than by fatigue from the long march. At night the unmarried made fun of their married comrades, and the more experienced soldiers either recounted their exploits or went out marauding together.

After the men had had a chance to rest in Radkersburg, Isakovič started subjecting them to strenuous drills on the road. He taught them to run with pistols in their hands and knives in their teeth; he had them band together and storm tree trunks, shooting at them or hacking off their branches while chanting the name of Maria Theresa in unison. When they got to the crest of a hill, he made them race down into the valley, shouting, and when they got to the valley, he made them race up the next hill, shouting, always with a standard-bearer in front. When they came to bridges, he divided them into two opposing groups and personally incited one against the other, twisting and turning wildly on his horse amid the flashing scimitars and smoking gunpowder, amid roaring masses of savage, blood-thirsty men. And when they pitched camp for the night, he made them dig ditches and lie beside them, then he had barrels of gunpowder rolled into the ditches and set on fire.

Weary as they were, they climbed the densely wooded hills. There were days when they forded the meandering Mur five times. More like birds than men, they scaled hills in whose shadow they peered down on the fields, villages, churches and vineyards they had left behind; they passed beneath enormous cliffs with pure, murmuring streams rushing down them, the fresh cold air cutting into their breasts like a knife. Many fell ill.

They wondered at the towns carved out of stone, at strange bridges, at devices whose use they could not fathom, at mountains of scythes that had been sold to Russian merchants. They heard music whose source they could not identify, because it came through walls. They saw a house with a blacksmith on the roof, a blacksmith made of iron yet alive, because he kept raising a hammer in his iron hands and pounding it on an anvil. Some crossed themselves and gaped; others removed their pipes from their mouths and spat indignantly, certain there was villainy involved.

The air made them drunk.

The land in which they had lived – flat and boggy, a land of fog and warm vapours, of waving reeds and weeping willows, of muddy dugouts and pigsties, of wooden churches – had all but vanished from their memory. The new land – green and cold, a land of dark forests, of clearings with the sky glittering like a deep, transparent lake overhead – chased the other land, the windy land, away. Heads low, they inhaled, imbibed the splendid mountains, unable to believe their eyes when in the distance they spied a rim of snow. Filthy and miserable, they passed stone homesteads bursting with hay and livestock, and felt the enormity of their destitution, the immensity of the mire in which they had lived.

When they were welcomed with feasts, with roasted goats and wine by the vat, with church bells, they could not help noting the difference between their misery at home and the joys of others. Their own land – its lazy, turgid rivers, its islands of henbane and poppies, elders and poplars, its frogs croaking – had receded into the realm of dreams; the people they had left behind appeared to them only as grimy scraps of memory.

On the outskirts of villages they passed huge stoves, foundries. Workers dressed in leather, sooty and singed, black as devils, ran out to have a look at them. The great fires in the furnaces, lighting up whole hillsides in the evening, lit their bivouacs as well, filling their dreams with strange red beasts – flaming bulls and buffalo – and seething water, a true inferno.

Bumptious and brazen early in the march, they withdrew into despondency on foreign soil. They no longer had the strength to crush everything in their path, and they no longer dared touch the women. When they came to a village, they would huddle together in a crowd, timid, humble, submissive, ready to accept any offer of friendship. No tamer soldiers had ever been seen in those parts. They were worn down further by the daily drills in the woods and meadows. By the time they entered Graz, they were pale and emaciated, their eyes bloodshot; yet they amazed the population with the brilliance of their arms, specially polished for the occasion, with their famous running charge, and their chanting. A messenger was sent to the Empress when they left Graz.

Drained from working his men so hard, Vuk Isakovič entered Austria suffering severe stomach pains. He was frequently forced to dismount, leave the company of his officers, and take refuge, behind the cloud of dust raised by the men, in a cart, which jolted him like a corpse or an enormous wineskin filled to the brim. Bringing up the rear of the regiment, he let the world go by as if it were a dream. He had spent many years in the army and was accustomed to riding to battle in a cart. Riding in a cart seemed to follow some inexorable rule, an alien will in an alien land.

Though without any ties in these parts, he kept coming upon traces of previous soldiers and traces of himself as well: in towns where he had watched the sun rise or laid his head down at night or, only a few years before, strolled along the ramparts and moonlit paths like a spectre. He recognized the smugglers and ferrymen, the discarded women, his own and his comrades', and the sites of both reveries and misfortunes. Now, riding along on a sunny day, exhausted from stomach pains, dozing, he had visions of familiar barns, rows of houses filled with the sick, moaning wounded soldiers, rainy nights.

Yet so crushed was he that he no longer cared about anything. Not so much because they had insulted and humiliated him at Pécs as because they had failed to promote him to lieutenant colonel, which he at his age had every right to expect, and which he had been promised in Varadin.

He felt the rupture from his wife and children to be complete, though he could not keep from thinking about them. If someone had whispered in his ear that he no longer had a wife and children, he would have believed him, so alone did he feel in the cart, where he could hardly stretch out full length because of all the hats, braiding, kettles, and saddles. As he thought of his family, he realized how dependent he was on others, that is, on those responsible for moving him from place to place in all his finery, and on his men, whom the dust had reduced to a crowd of feet marching in step.

The world beyond the cart ceased to exist for him – the woods, the clearings, the valleys, and he felt he was being mindlessly, hopelessly jolted off in some arbitrary direction. Yet he could hear the swift rhythm of the men's step, the clank of their arms; he could hear a mighty chant, in unison, of the syllables Ma-ri-a, Ma-ri-a, The-re-sa, The-re-sa. And he could feel the warm air as they passed through open fields, and the refreshing breezes as they entered a wood.

Although he had made precise provision for all needs until the fighting started, both food and money had begun to dwindle and the men to fall ill from the water. He envied his officers, who did not need to worry about such things, and his men, who did not even know where they were going. The weeping and wailing that accompanied their departure now seemed sensible to him, and he had a strong feeling that this would be his last campaign, that in this battle he would fall.

His mood changed suddenly, inexplicably. He would be riding out in front of the regiment with the officers, smoking his pipe, when for no reason he would jump into a cart and jolt along behind the regiment. Or he would be cheerfully swaying in time to a song, his hat at a rakish angle, when he would gallop off with a kick to his mount.

Now, moaning with pain in the cart, he felt as if it had been raining for days, raining endlessly, washing away not only his wife and children but his life, everything he had known. Watching the clouds sail past the peaks, he felt that the peaks too were washing down on him, vast streams of rock against fields of deep, white snow and the giant shadows of the cliffs.

As the cart climbed behind the troops through the fir wood, the land and villages below disappeared from sight. The creaking of the wheels lulled him, as did the constant crackle of twigs and fir needles that coated the mountain with a soft, mosslike bed so thick that the wheels sank in up to the hub.

The mountain crests, shrouded in a silence that not even the troops could disturb, remained visible the entire day, and Isaković never took his eyes off them. Like the crests of huge waves their snow-swept crags loomed closer and closer, tumbling into the valleys along the thickly shadowed slopes, where they dispersed into forests of fir overgrown with tall grass that inundated everything – stumps, stones, streams – like a flood-tide.

The thought that his death was imminent made Vuk Isaković despondent. Robust and hearty as he was, he saw himself as weak, even feeble, and lying in the cart, riding behind the troops, he succumbed even more to the absurd sadness of it all. As he gazed up at the colossal heights, at the blue shadows in the snow, and rode through the warm spring day and fir-tree fragrance, his whole life passed before him. Next to the terrifyingly massive mountains and the firs, whose branches spread like birds of prey ready to descend the slopes, his life seemed very light and airy, ready to take flight.

Whenever he felt tired, he would stop the cart and lie down alongside the road among the stumps, exposing his aching stomach to the sun and observing for hours, his hat pulled over his brow, the ants that swarmed around his head. At other times his thoughts so ran away with him that he imagined watching himself as he lay in the cart, in the straw, or sitting at his own feet under the firs, staring at his enormous boots, his tightly clad haunches, his open lace-trimmed shirt, his hirsute chest, his silver braid, his double chins and flat nose. He imagined peering into his own large, bulging yellowish eyes and seeing the black greatcoat stretched around him. He imagined having a conversation with himself.

His youth stopped coming back to him, and when he tried to recall it, it grew dim and vanished, leaving him invariably with the images of his wife and children. Nor could he call forth the golden age he had experienced during the Turkish Wars; it kept merging with places where he had lived with his wife and where his children had been born. At so many removes nothing made sense.

His wife, who bored him, and children, who belonged to him, followed him about like distant shadows. Whether he returned home or not, he would feel from now on that he had broken with them forever. What good was a family if he could not do as he wished for them, if he was obliged to turn this way and that like a weathercock at someone else's will? Attired as he was, did he not belong to others more than to his wife and children who cried for him – to those who with a mere nod could send him anywhere, not stopping to ask whether it caused him suffering or what horrors he left behind or madness he ran towards?

Living at the mercy of others, was he not condemned to leaving scraps of his existence in houses of towns where he would never set foot again? Was he not accustomed to leaving when he would stay and staying when he would leave? Even now, before death kept him from going where he pleased and where people were pleased to have him, even now, in the midst of life, he was unable to return to the places where he had lived several years in succession and where he wished to live again. Did anyone know he had experienced the most gentle awakening of spring twelve years before, while living near the Osijek fortress, or the most silent silence of night near the town of Varadin, where he had settled? No one had ever asked. And his way now led neither to Osijek nor to Varadin, but in the opposite direction. Was it not in vain, then, that he had lain motionless for months near a tributary of the Danube with a frightful wound that went from his Adam's apple to his right shoulder, hovering between life and death, his eyes filled with the yellow light of the floodwater, the sand, and the tips of the poplars? Three years later he had passed through the place again, to find that no one recalled so much as his name, and a Walachian woman he had loved well and paid well failed to recognize him.

His heavy cart would catch up with the regiment when it stopped to rest near a village or near a bridge, or when the officers decided to amuse themselves by riding to hounds or attending the dances given in their honour. At night he would choose a place overlooking the troops, who dotted the woods with their fires. Lit by the flames, the men looked like beasts. The road, winding higher and higher among the still-light mountaintops, eventually vanished in the dusk, and the dense, bushy trees along the edge of the woods cast ever longer shadows across the grass. Soon the village where he could have spent the night looked like nothing more than a heap of stones in the bed of a dried-up stream.

Above the village darkness came later than it did to the meadow crisscrossed by streams and rows of trees. Here and there he could make out a lone house that looked like a stump, or a tall, ungainly bear of a tree. Beyond were dense woods again and, like huge stone curtains, the crags, peaks, precipitous slopes. Up there the sky remained light until close to midnight, when it came alive with numberless pale stars, which diminished at dawn but went on shining.

Settling down near a fir, usually the tallest, he would surround himself with his dogs and grumble into the night long after everyone around him was asleep. He would turn his back to the fire, for warmth in the spring night. He had been treating his stomach with a cure recommended by his servant: fasting and keeping it warm with sheepskins, wine, and *rakija*.

It was on such a night that the thought first came to him, as it had come to his men, the thought of not returning home. The intimation of death, which he had never experienced before when setting off to war, now joined the boredom he always felt until the fighting began. After running through the list of ailing soldiers and lame horses in his mind, he cursed those of sound body with no less contempt, though not before cursing himself. Constant drilling and warring had made him such a master of leading men into battle that he foresaw exactly what would happen, even the slightest mishap. He may have erred about an occasional headstrong Walachian stallion or massive Austrian mare prone to unpredictable vagaries, but he never erred in the choice of carts, wheels, or men. The shortage of food did not particularly bother him now, though they would have to forage; all that mattered was to deliver the men to their goal. Then he could fall in battle.

In his weary state, the idea of not returning home and not having to deal with the men seemed so extraordinary as to be impossible. Would he never cease kicking those enormous

83

feet that could not march in step, or beating those backs and bellies that refused to straighten when presenting arms? If only he did not have to beat them when they stared dumbly at kegs of gunpowder instead of setting them afire, if only he did not have to slap them, punch them, kick them. And, most of all, if only he did not have to return home and face the weeping and wailing, the half-crazed women tearing at their breasts, keening, howling, mourning their dead.

He had come to loathe the land they had left behind, the land where he had left his family. He had been commanded to teach his men not only to dig trenches but also to drain swamps, and while teaching them to shoot a salvo – which he never succeeded in doing – he also taught them to put up walls on the dry ground near the swamps and willows where they lived and died on their haunches in bushes and underbrush, dugouts and lean-tos. It was a stupid place, stupid, water-logged, boggy, flat; he could not stand it any longer, and would have left long ago had he had the chance.

Although he had become skilled in military arts, he scorned them, as he scorned the Gypsylike nomads, who – unlike the Walachian Gypsies, whose young girls, in his memory, smelled of roses – were coarse and poor and lived off Turkey's rubbish heaps. In his fury he would gladly have taken the entire region he had traversed with his father and brother and set it on fire or sold it, along with the people around Varadin, whom he personally had settled there and who worshipped him. But even when compassion took the place of fury, which it did as impetuously as fury took the place of compassion, even then he wished to remove the people from that place, from that life.

At such times, desperately confused, he would think of his brother, his sickly brother, and was grateful to him for watching over his wife and daughters, yet raged against him as one rages against an absent party. All the man's petty buying and selling now seemed absurd. Yet having to make peace with him before setting off, he had failed to receive not only the money owed him but his wife's money as well, and was forced in addition to put up with his brother's snicker at the idea of a new migration, to Russia perhaps.

The life he lived at home was no life for Vuk Isakovič; real life, a life of beauty and consequence, was elsewhere. Life at home was all swamps and poverty and the filthy back alleys that Arandjel said were worth their weight in smiles, transactions, and gold. Vuk would rather have closed his eyes to all of it, not to mention Turkey, where some of their acquaintances had turned. Turkey was a place Vuk Isakovič despised, having no eyes for its cobblestone courtyards, its fine fountains and bridges, its tall and stately lancelike minarets.

To go off and lead a carefree existence, taking his men with him and giving them a pleasant, easy life, suddenly seemed possible. There had to be a proper place somewhere; they had only to find it. He would take them there, he thought, leaning against a wheel and surveying the dark mass of men below him as they lay in the grass around the carts, their faces illuminated by the fires. For a moment he forgot where he was and where he was bound for, and staring up at the steep faces of rock and at the limpid, pale blue sky, he made his peace with the men of the Slavonian-Danubian Regiment.

They were all asleep. As the pain in his gut abated, he too dozed, stroking his dogs, who rubbed up against him and stuck their muzzles under his sheepskin jacket to keep warm. Beneath the trees behind the cart he could hear the rumination of the cattle that had been brought from Graz for the officers, and beyond the trees the chirping of crickets. But proving that the route to Bavaria that he had chosen was superior to the one proposed by Count Serbelloni, the general of the cavalry, was his foremost concern. And so, his stomach having calmed down, he decided to wake the troops early and proceed immediately in the direction of the Danube.

*

The men were glad to descend into Austria's valleys, orchards, and rich plains: they were better fed now and, because speed was of the essence, drilled less often. The days were one long march in double columns; the nights, loud snoring. Villagers held dances for the Serbs passing through, and landowners invited them to masked balls. In better spirit, the men began to sing again, especially when they came to towns that offered good wine in abundance. Many of the sick left their carts. And when, at Krems, they sighted the Danube, which they all dearly loved, they began to run, as they had from Srem to Pécs, to run and shout and break down fences.

But not long after, their spirits sank again: Bavaria was poor and starving.

Once more Vuk Isakovič rode out in front with his fat, indolent orderly Arkadije – known to the entire regiment as a great drunkard and a great singer – and his officers, who smoked their pipes and sang, while the men behind them droned in a hundred variations, drawing out the final e . . . ei . . . e . . . ei . . .

Although scarcely able to pull their feet out of the soggy soil, the men managed to reach Ingolstadt, on the Danube, with all their carts intact. There the regiment was to be joined by great masses of Austrian troops and a force of their own men from the Military Frontier.

They arrived from the south at dawn, and as they were about to ford the river and parade through the town, they saw hands waving at them from the far bank and heard drunken curses unknown in this part of the world but familiar and affectionate to them. The men on the other side of the river, just awakened and still in their underwear, belonged to the two regiments led by Lieutenant Colonel Arsenije Vuič. The soldiers felt as if they were home again, and their spirits rose.

The men from the Military Frontier under the command of Lieutenant Captain Ivan Horvat had not yet arrived. All that was known of them was that they were raising hell in Lower Bavaria.

For two weeks Isakovič bivouacked with Vuič's troops – they were worse than his – outside Ingolstadt, after which each of the commanders set off with his men for the Rhine by a different but predetermined route.

Isakovič decided he would have his men file past him and catch up with them in the final stretch. They were annoyed at having set off last, and he made matters worse by putting them through their paces as they forded the river. But in this way he succeeded in uniting them for the goal at which all his earlier drills were aimed: massacre and death. Back to back and in squares, the units had advanced and shot, ever steadier, more unbending and menacing, as though bewitched by his shouts. During the previous two days he had borrowed the cavalry from the neighbouring camp and let them loose on his men, swords waving, horses rearing, the earth trembling beneath their hooves. The moment he sensed revolt or retreat, there he was, club in hand.

From Bavaria, which was considered enemy territory, he entered Württemberg. Its fragrant forests and hills having burst into bloom, he began searching for a place to store the skins, coats, and blankets the men had hauled on their backs all the way from home. Spring was in full force, and a hot summer was in the offing.

After a good night's sleep in the grass, which despite the fine spring mist mantling the budding meadows was at dawn no longer wet, the men would march the whole day, pausing only for the midday meal in steep town squares and taking the evening meal in mountain villages, where, tired though they were, they danced in the moonlight. The acacias were intoxicating; insects buzzed through the night.

Having pushed his men to the limit, Isakovič now – as the end was approaching – allowed them some respite. The sentries were not so strict at night, and if a soldier was late for morning roll call, he received no more than a mild clubbing. Not until local peasants began dragging in dead-drunk veterans of the Turkish Wars, not until his own orderly Arkadije disappeared and was found two days later dressed in several layers of skirts – not until then did he change tactics: the regiment started sleeping by day and marching by the light of the moon.

The two weeks spent at Ingolstadt with Vuič's regiments had disheartened him, for there he had heard that his promotion to the rank of lieutenant colonel was out of the question, that in fact the authorities were extremely displeased with the Military Frontier regiments. There had been talk at headquarters of abolishing them altogether and distributing the men among regular regiments. The cuirassiers, peruked to a man, gave them an icy reception, and one of his officers, Captain Antonovič, was forced to draw his sword in order to keep a table at an inn where the cuirassiers were entertaining two Italian actresses. In the eyes of these bedecked and bedizened imperial officers, the Serbian nation, privileged as it was by the Empress, was a proper target for mockery – but otherwise a blank, an obscure thing, in whose existence they did not feel the need to believe.

The food supplied to the Serbs was the worst in the army. When Vuič threatened to complain to Vienna, the authorities took his horses and then the cart with gunpowder he had bought with funds his regiments had carried with them from the Military Frontier. To make matters worse, they were required to stand guard for the entire camp, which meant that his men were on duty day and night, while the others could come and go in the town as they pleased.

Like the rest of them, Isakovič could only gnash his teeth. He felt betrayed. He had his own ideas about this army, which they had all rushed to join but which in the end had little use for the men from the swamps, who had their own special prayers, monks, synods, laments, and their "sweet Orthodoxy". Moreover, approaching a field of battle for the fourth time, he suspected that things would not improve, that his men would be sent to serve in other regiments, and that on their return home they would be divided between landowners and towns as servants, as serfs; they would not be allowed to remain soldiers, nor would they be allowed to have their own churches, just as they had not been allowed to call their country New Serbia. That is why he became even more lenient during the last stretch. He would watch his men in silence, their feet, their faces, watch the clouds of dust they raised, the dust to which they would soon return. He remained silent for days, watching them, sparing them, knowing they would soon die and disperse, like smoke after a battle.

His heart went out to other regiments as well – to Vuič's men, who came from villages along the Sava and the Drava. The futility of his life, the folly of having a wife and children and a home to return to, of everything he was doing, grew clearer to him the more he watched the men trudging deaf and dumb through foreign lands with no idea where they were being led. Weak with humiliation, he suffered frequent bile attacks; his blood would rush to his head for no reason. Muttering to himself, barely moving his mustachio, he was uncomfortable in his saddle. Unlike the officers in front of him, who, delighted by the richness of the spring, paused to admire every inn, every orchard, every wrought-iron castle gate overgrown with ivy, and the acacias and small prickly roses, he rode on as if lost, surly, sallow, swollen, his head bobbing above his enormous stomach, his brain a muddle of letters to Patriarch Šakabenta, petitions to the Court, quarrels with his brother, Arandjel, and desperately bitter self-recrimination. Thus he saw neither the petals falling from the fruit trees like fragrant rain nor the people streaming through the streets or flocking to their windows to marvel at his huge sturdy mount, his gaily singing officers, their unsheathed swords and their strange, peasant dress all of the same cut and colour.

Word of the presence of Maria Theresa's army spread quickly through the Principality of Württemberg, which was generally acknowledged to be a potential theatre of war. While awaiting the arrival of the French – the subject of lively discussion, especially among the ladies – many turned out to see the Serbs, who they assumed would flee, defeated and shamed, the moment the fighting began. Yet not a day passed but that they were feted with a dance, where beer flowed in an endless stream, or a dinner, where by lantern light in the church square they ate themselves into a stupor.

The day after they crossed the border, a courier presented Major Isakovič with a message from Prince Karl Eugen of Württemberg, requesting him to follow Vuič directly, as His Royal Highness the Prince wished to review the Serbian troops that had so faithfully served under his glorious father, the late Karl Alexander, Field Marshal of the Empire, Conqueror of Temesvár, Governor of Serbia, etc., etc. He made a special point of the fact that the Princess Mother, who had withdrawn from society after her husband's death and taken up residence with her son, had expressed the desire to see the Serbian troops again.

The troops were overjoyed at the news: they immediately pictured oxen on the spit, kegs of beer, and at least two days of sleep. Isakovič, however, felt a sudden strange confusion. While the troops slept along the river, he sat in his saddle gazing at the glimmering water, as stunned as a fisherman would be on finding incredible new varieties of red, green, and silver fish wriggling in his net. The days ahead flashed before his eyes.

At home he had a portrait of Karl Alexander of Württemberg framed in silver, enamel, and tourmaline, which he had received as a gift while in the Prince's service at the Belgrade fortress. He could see it clearly, a miniature likeness supported by a baroque Hercules brandishing a club and by a Mars with a wailing Medusa on his shield, and surmounted by a winged and magnificently pink-breasted Victory puffing on a clarion. Drums, maces, axes, horse tails, and half-crescent standards lay strewn before the Prince, who was all wig, puckered lips, and armour.

That image was followed by others still alive in his memory from the days when the Danubian Regiment waged war from the fortress at Belgrade against the Turks. As both the youngest officer and the Prince's favourite, he was often asked to wait on him. His duties were arduous and of a highly personal nature, ranging from the bedchamber to the money-changing booths operated by Greeks and Jews, who even working together were hard put to satisfy the Prince's needs. He also served at the Prince's gaming tables, where familiarity with martingale was essential. His various duties were not easy, even though his main duty was to stand in silence holding a candle.

Vuk Isakovič was not disturbed by his memories of the Prince, whom he thought of as a grotesque monster with a habit of grabbing a button of Vuk's uniform and holding it until he had finished what he had to say, breathing into Vuk's mouth the while. But what did confuse and disturb him, covered with dust as he was, his lips drooping, his Turkish trousers baggy, was his memory of the Princess Mother, now the widow of Karl Alexander but then a woman in her prime. He remembered her silk shoes with heels five inches high, and her breasts, which glowed pink, like Victory's in the Prince's portrait.

6

The Past Is Terrifying, an Abyss;
All That Enters into Its Darkness Ceases to Exist,
nor Did It Ever Exist

No, Vuk Isakovič had never been the lover of the wife of Prince Karl Alexander of Württemberg. The truth is she had no lovers while in Belgrade.

Observing the well-built young officer standing guard before her husband's door, she soon realized he constantly stared at her with great admiration, timidity, and longing – as if she were a heavenly being. And because she found it so amusing, she began staring back, as one eyes a cat one has tossed a ball of wool to. She told her husband she considered him a child, even though Isakovič, standing at attention in his uniform, resembled a solid block of wood.

She took to strutting back and forth in front of him, turning to inspect her skirts, finding something to brush off, a bit of fluff, a speck of dust visible only to her, or standing at the window in his presence, above the ramparts, looking down at the confluence of the Sava and the Danube, or up, like an angel, at the evening sky, yet watching him out of the corner of her eye as she prattled to her ladies-in-waiting. It was her wish to seem sublime, inviolate. Although she had a grown son, she wanted the young savage from that strange land to think her as pure and unattainable as a virgin. She succeeded.

Every morning when he reported for duty, she would

appear as if by chance, wearing a low-cut dress and no wig – her short curly hair black as the devil – and train her lorgnette in his direction, whereupon he stood stock-still, turned pale and wide-eyed. When he was invited to dine at the Prince's table, she ignored him, said not a word to him. He, for his part, had to hide his trembling hands under the table.

And so a secret bond was established between them during that first spring of her sojourn in Belgrade.

Isaković had been initiated into the desires of the heart by a number of women, the most notable among them a French actress from Temesvár, and he knew exactly what was expected of him. Yet he was terrified. He thought of the Princess as completely different from others – exquisite, ethereal, sublime. Not one of his fellow officers would have dared, would have dreamed of paying suit to her, though word of their amorous exploits had reached the Court. He had seen her silk slippers and gold-embroidered stockings, her shoulders and ripe, peach-coloured knees when he helped her on to her mount, but everything about her was so different. He was sure she would have died had she been able to read his thoughts. Other Serbs who occasionally had the honour of dining with her were of the same opinion.

When playing cards at her table, which he did almost nightly, he counted himself lucky to touch, unnoticed, the gloves she had removed, or to run his hand furtively over her cape. Although he, like his fellow officers, had had to learn to dance, and was indeed a fine dancer, she never chose him as a partner; so when the sweet viols began to play, he was obliged to bow to some old crone in her entourage – they all adored him. After these soirées he and his friends would carouse till dawn, singing to the gusla at the top of their lungs and bursting with eloquence and vitality.

The ravages of love and desire soon took their toll, however, and his friends began to notice how gaunt he looked. When, on the strength of his spotless record and reputation for bravery, the Prince requested him to tame and train a herd of Walachian horses, Isakovič had to suffer not only by night – in solitude and silence, near her boudoir, listening for her footsteps, watching her maids run out with dresses and in with nightshirts – but also by day, dizzy with the fragrance of the grass and earth kicked up by the horses as they rode together. One morning she nearly fell from her horse, and pressed against him with all her weight when he raced up to her aid.

Awkward and humble, Isakovič went through nearly half a year of infernal torture, all but unable to look at a woman other than the stately, sweet-scented, extraordinary Princess. Inflamed to the brink of madness, he received the news of preparation for an attack on the Turks in early autumn as a message from heaven: the Princess would be leaving Belgrade for Temesvár. He had never, not with the slightest gesture or turn of phrase, dared to allude to his passion, and he was pleased by the prospect of shedding the constant burden it had become. Although she was his first true love, she had entered his life just as his father began to talk of finding him a bride.

His relief at her departure was of course mixed with horror at the thought he might never see her again, and he gazed upon her so wide-eyed and despondent that her feeling of superiority began to wane. During her last few days in Belgrade, she scarcely knew what to do with him. She wondered whether she had not gone too far, and whether she should not in fact grant him some favour, this young officer whom she liked to picture leading a band of brigands in the mountains. Yet for all her regret, she could not find the proper occasion to act upon it.

One September morning, on her way to see her husband, who was settling accounts with some Greeks and shouting so loudly that she could hear his voice two halls away, she spied the mustachioed officer. She paused, removed her wig, shook out her hair, and walked past him back to her room. He dutifully aimed his rifle at the floor until she had closed the door behind her.

A swarm of flies buzzed at her window, which looked out over the moss-covered ramparts to grassy plains stretching north, reeds lining the riverbanks, and military vessels with large green sails plying the river, a cannon gaping out of every shadow. The cloud-laden sky hung over the water like a huge damp sheet.

Standing at the window, she called him in and, fingering a small gold cross that drew his eyes to the pink cleft between her breasts, inquired whether her coach and young Count Patašič, who was accompanying her to Temesvár, had arrived. Then she approached him and, looking deep into his eyes for the first time, asked whether his duties would be bringing him to Temesvár, which was much more pleasant than Belgrade, or to Vienna, where she planned to winter, or to Württemberg, where she could show him her appreciation for his loyalty to her husband. Her words coming to an end, she gave him so wanton a smile that he felt his knees buckle. As if distracted, she leaned out of the window, above the ramparts and moats, and, dropping the chain with the cross, let out a muffled cry.

Isakovič ran to her, solicitous, out of breath. Careful to see that no one was coming – her husband's chambers were two halls away – she asked him to lean out and look for the chain in the grass. The window was narrow, and he pressed hard against the wall, constrained as by a coat of mail, to avoid touching her body. But she also leaned out of the window, repeated her request, and even grabbed his hand, which was cold as a corpse's. Grazing his chest as she turned her head, she felt for the first time what it was like to be close to him, what she now had and would soon lose. At that moment Vuk Isakovič was a handsome man with feverish eyes the colour of ancient gold and livid lips beneath the exotic glossy-black serpentine coils of his mustachio. He was deathly pale and

95

absolutely still. Feeling bitter and tearful, she did not leave her rooms again that day.

Toward evening she learned that her carriage had arrived and that she would be departing in two days.

Waking the next morning – a lovely warm morning – the sight of a large coach in the courtyard made the Princess sick with rage. Now that she could go at last, she wanted desperately to stay, if only to spend an hour with him undisturbed. She yearned to bask now under the blue Oriental sky she had always found so tedious – the sky, the ramparts, the mud, the same fish on the table day in and day out, the same talk. He was so different from her husband and from all her former lovers – dark, silent, his soul more submissive yet more ample, like his body.

After torturing herself for some time, she determined to have him made part of her entourage or guard, or have him transferred to Temesvár, and all morning she minced snake-like before her husband and his senior officers. By noon, however, she had resigned herself to her fate and, weeping bitterly, let her companions and servants sprinkle her with water, rub her back, and dress her. At the same time they made ready for the journey and delivered a message from the young Count Patašič, who was said to be very handsome. He duly inquired as to whether she preferred him to ride alongside the coach or sit with her and keep her company.

Later, she thought about what had passed between her and Isakovič the day before, and beside herself, burning with desire, vanity, and spite, she dismissed the guard in front of Isakovič's door and burst into his room, which was on that day particularly dirty, to find him inspecting a saddle bought for the Prince from a Turk. He was in a dark mood, half asleep, bewildered by her presence, and before he could get to his feet, she ordered him to open the window. Then she sidled up to him with an insolent smile, leaned out over the ramparts and the river as she had the day before, and looked him straight in the eye – his gaze was cloudy and sunken – and asked whether the soldiers had found her chain.

It was warmer that day, muggy, overcast. Rain was in the air. She asked whether he saw anything in the grass. And moving closer, she could feel his knees and thighs through her soft light riding skirts. Looking over the scorched yet stiflingly aromatic meadow and the overripe river plants, as if searching for the chain, she thrust herself between him and the wall. The silence was complete. As he leaned against her, his body trembling, she covered her face with her hands and pressed closer until, overcome, she too began to tremble. Her head was spinning. It was an exquisite sensation.

But just as she was about to turn and face him, she gasped for breath and slipped into a dead faint.

Vuk Isakovič mulled over this event, in various places and for many years, until he gradually forgot about it.

Now, thirty years later, that woman resurfaced in his memory – she and the fortress overlooking the Danube and his comrades in the old Danubian Regiment, and he remembered that autumn and his youth – and though he had not sought her out, he would have to see her: she was waiting for him in a town where his troops were expected. As the meeting, on this oddly familiar foreign soil, came closer, he kept thinking of ways to avoid the inevitable.

Meanwhile, courier after courier delivered greetings and invitations from the Prince and the Princess Mother.

"I should never have recognized you," said the Princess Mother of Karl Eugen of Württemberg after the grand welcome. Vuk Isakovič stood stiffly before her in his dress tunic, white gloves reaching to his elbows and red Turkish trousers that drooped both front and back. "You have changed so, aged so."

He smiled awkwardly, as if troubled by a guilty conscience.

97

He was further embarrassed by the thought that her words could be heard by a group of Serbian officers breathing deeply and loudly on his hair and neck, embarrassed by the sight of his own image in the mirror the Princess Mother was standing near. The mirror, tall as a gate, also gave him a view of the gilt and milk-white walls, the ceiling of opalescent angels and pink-kneed shepherds in turned-up tunics, the copper candelabra embossed with minute cherubs and leaves, and finally the Princess Mother herself, whom he saw thus mirrored, from the back, before looking her in the face.

She was dressed like a young girl. Part of her hair was piled high on her head and bound with a white ribbon; the rest hung down her back in a braid. Her bare shoulders, their furrows packed with white powder, shone like dry bones in the sun. Her back was straight, laced as it was into armour made of silk, and her waist, as firm and round as the trunk of an old pear tree, seemed to serve no other purpose than to hold up a series of petticoats – a voluminous tent hung with branches and garlands and which had nothing whatever inside.

After gazing upon this chimera, Vuk saw his own comrades – whom the mirror showed immobile beside a large wooden clock, its pendulum swinging back and forth, bright and yellow, sunlike – and they looked like painted dolls, with their slicked-down hair, their lace and gold braid, their hats held over their hearts. For a moment he lost track of where he was.

When he looked up at the Princess Mother again, this time face to face, he was surprised to see her dressed in pink and white lace with a double row of embroidery at the bodice and sleeves that from the elbow down practically became skirts. She had a large feather fastened by pearl stickpins to her coiffure, a blue ribbon tied in a bow under her chin, and a bouquet of flowers attached to her left shoulder. Her neck was a mass of wrinkles, and just to the left of her décolletage ran a long, sinuous, thin blue vein. By tightly binding her breasts, which were so large it must have caused discomfort, she was able to give her chest a pleasing if oddly flat appearance. She continuously waved a fan decorated with tiny birds and lambs and containing a tiny watch in the handle. Her fingers were gnarled, her hands covered with thick veins.

His eyes bulging, Vuk stared at her decrepit face, its wattled chin, drooping ears, and bright-red cheeks beneath a layer of white powder generously dotted with false beauty spots. Her nose consisted of three mounds, a top and two splayed nostrils; her eyebrows, of two crooked, malevolent lines. All that remained of her once dark beauty were the large eyes, but even they had receded into pits of skin, bags, and creases, with white patches and impurities of every kind.

She looked him over with a sardonic smile: she too was surprised, by his stooped frame, sagging mouth, listless mustachio, tired eyes. What irritated her most was that he kept shifting from foot to foot. She – and not only she – saw him as hollow, an empty barrel with clothes on.

Much as she wished to be pleasant, she expressed only contempt and scorn. She looked him up and down several times more as he presented his officers to her one by one. Hearing her voice and silent laughter, he felt awkward, chilled to the knees, though his forehead was beaded with sweat.

At last she turned to her son, the Prince, who stood behind her, looking on in admiration with his suite of ladies, courtiers, and cuirassiers. He was wearing a white powdered wig with a black bow at the neck, great quantities of lace, and a breastplate. "Look at these gentlemen," she said in a loud voice, so that everyone could hear. "They are tried and true. They served valiantly under my late husband and were always loyal and devoted to him, for which he vouchsafed them his love and respect."

The Prince was fingering a watch chain in his left hand – his eyes rooted to the charms that hung from it, cupids, mythological goddesses, and flowers – and tugging at his breastplate with his right. He was aware that his mother had put him in the embarrassing position of having to say something, and that everyone was staring in his direction; yet he could not bring forth a word. Luckily, the Princess Mother immediately resumed her speech, looking at the Serbs with deep emotion. "This is the happiest day of my life, for I have been granted the privilege of seeing once more the men who have always, in all circumstances, supported us and remained faithful." And as she thought back to the days she had spent in Serbia at her husband's side, tears welled up in her eyes and she was unable to refrain from crying.

Accustomed to acting upon the orders of their commander – and aware of the rumours about his acquaintance with the Princess Mother – the officers looked to Isakovič. They were in no more enviable a position than he – polished, pomaded, stuffed into new sashes, jingling at every step. In the glow of hundreds upon hundreds of candles they felt unable to conceal the marks of the rains they had marched through, the nights they had spent in huts and under carts, the weeks of marshes, filth, and negligence. The parquet floors made them uneasy, as did the half-naked statues that adorned the alcoves where they would have liked to hide. The decorous courtiers, who proposed a round at the gaming tables, looked outlandish to them in their perfumed wigs, silk stockings, long velour jackets, and with their sprig-slim swords. The ladies, who inquired what it was like to sleep in the open, appeared equally strange: great shrubs of hair, flowers, feathers, painted faces, bared breasts, and skirts so wide they had to take care not to upset the alabaster vases on the gueridons. For the officers and their commander, then, the evening was long and arduous, and they stuck together, bowing, smiling, making polite, red-faced conversation, yet always ready to decamp. Many friendships started during the march were cemented that evening on the basis of the common ordeal.

The courtiers had been ordered to explain the views of their young Prince concerning the delicate position of Württemberg in the military maelstrom, that is, its position vis-à-vis Vienna, which was ruled by a woman, after all, and to urge the officers on to great feats by glorifying the friendship between Württemberg and the Serbs, sealed in blood and significant for a number of reasons, the most important being that it would spread the Serbs' fame the world over and that it was God's will. The officers were less than moved by the courtiers' tributes, their attention having turned to the gaming tables.

Captain Antonovič, the richest among them and a master gambler, had warned them in advance of the wiles they could expect, especially from the women who would be sitting at their sides. And in fact many a local beauty, desirous of something different, spent the evening coquettishly batting her eyelashes and laughing behind her fan. The men ignored them; clasping their cards in one hand and their money in the other, they made jokes in Serbian at the women's expense, confident they would not be understood and could not therefore be outsmarted. As for the friendship between Serbia and Württemberg, they had their own ideas on the subject and between their teeth cursed Württemberg and everything with the slightest connection to Württemberg.

As time went on, however, they could not help being dazzled, blinded by the candles that blazed wildly in silver candelabra, by the glittering mirrors, the black lacquer gaming tables, the carvings, the marble fireplaces and silk tablecloths. So overwhelmed were they by the pomp and the proximity of perfumed half-naked women that they grew eager to shine, to show how rich they were, how expansive, good-natured, and lavish, and soon they almost tried to lose. Stuffing their mouths with sweets and their pockets with handkerchiefs and locks of hair passed under the table as souvenirs, they vied for the cards of the prettiest women. Captain Antonovič, who dealt out the hands and raked in the gold, berated them in vain: they were finally at their ease, enjoying themselves; they pushed tables over and rocked in chairs until they cracked like nutshells.

When, later, the French windows were opened and they gazed out at the elongated shadows of evening that made their way up the steps from deserted paths lined with newly pruned and blossoming trees to a row of white pillars, they felt renewed by a cool, pleasant breeze and a sky of a gentle, watery hue. Although they were no less fragile than the glass of the large French windows an arm's reach from their tables – thin, brittle, ready to shatter at the mere touch of an elbow, sword, or piece of furniture – not one of them thought that he was near death, that in the next few days he might cease to be, like the decorations that had been strung around the hall in their honour, the gilt paper and flowers and glass. Not one of them thought that he would leave behind nothing permanent, nothing of peace and beauty, like this evening stealing over the garden filled with an infinite number of lives now silent but ready to wake again at dawn. That he would leave, like the greyhounds out in the garden, nothing but a hairy coat, a stinking corpse, and, in the mud and misery that was home, a relative or two who might remember him for a time.

When Isakovič told them they would have to take their leave, they were indignant. The great mirrored hall had given them the sense of a fleeting stay in heaven, of rocking gently among the stars of the luminous Milky Way. After the dust that had filled their throats and noses and lodged in the furrows of their brows, after the mountains and rivers, marshes and orchards, hamlets and fences, courtyards and backyards they had crossed, they felt that they had come to a different world, a world where people spent their time, whole centuries, gazing at sunsets and gardens, magnificent fountains and extraordinarily beautiful, captivating, scented women in rooms filled with rosewood and silk and precious stones, and that all they had to do to savour a perfect sky, the finest jewels, divinely rounded breasts, silence, was extend a hand amid the moonlit mirrors.

Surrounded by women, delighted at being the centre of attention, they forgot their goal and their troubles for a moment, forgot that they had entered this new world not so many hours ago, and, as if it had been theirs forever, they were happy. After their initial reticence and churlish table manners, they had charmed Karl Eugen's retinue with their extravagance, good looks, and high spirits. They knew they were famous for their virility and were eager to demonstrate it to the German Empire. They also knew that Isakovič, along with the old Danubian Regiment, had been a great favourite at the court of Alexander of Württemberg, and they were hoping to see what mark he had left on the Princess Mother's memory. They were sadly disappointed – and so annoyed at having to leave that they took some satisfaction in noting how the Princess had seemed to avoid him and how he had grown more ponderous, more taciturn, more spent as the night progressed.

In fact, Vuk Isakovič was avoiding the Princess Mother, though she did not go out of her way to seek his company. He avoided looking at her face or even coming near her, the difference between what she was now and how he remembered her was so appalling. He spent the entire evening pacing the hall, distraught at having to endure this new trial, wanting nothing more than that it should end quickly. When it finally became time for him to say farewell, he gave her a rather less than elegant bow.

The Princess responded by announcing unexpectedly that she wished to see their camp, and he was obliged to promise that he would have everything ready for her by morning. She told him, with a tired smile not entirely free of malice, that she would send him some sheep and cows and several barrels of beer for the men, and some chickens and greens and wine for the officers. Then she held out her sinewy hand, under his nose, for a kiss.

*

And so Vuk Isakovič set off on the last stage of his journey to the tiny town of Stockstadt-on-the-Rhine, where he was awaited by Field Marshal Lieutenant Johann-Leopold Bärenklau, commander of the advance guard.

The French advance guard had taken up a position on the far side of the river, and was firing on and off, mostly at night.

The Austrian forces, having crossed enemy Bavaria, the Upper Palatinate, a vacillating Württemberg, Baden, and Hessen, had been gathering at a snail's pace throughout the spring of 1744. Their ultimate goal was to attack the French. Yet they could not help feeling iron Prussia breathing down their necks. Moreover, the commander sent by the Viennese Court, Prince Charles of Lorraine, was in no hurry to lead them. He treated them like huge flocks, driving them here and there, determined to bring every lost sheep back to the fold and show a benign face to any village or hamlet that would pledge allegiance to him. Even though the far side of the Rhine was his ancestral home, he had grown so accustomed to thinking in terms of Austria that he felt but little nostalgia for the hunting grounds, châteaux, or even the throne of his progenitors. He had rejoiced in the marriage of his brother Francis Stephen to Maria Theresa, assuming that his brother would one day wear the imperial crown of Austria.

He therefore had no qualms about leaving the French to battle it out with the English, and his experience in earlier wars had left him with nothing but scorn for Bavarians and their counter-emperor, Saxons, and all the rest; he did, however, fear the Prussians, who, although he considered himself a better commander than Frederick, more sophisticated if less fortunate, had defeated him several times. But then, Charles had more complicated tasks to perform: his battlefield stretched all the way from the Rhine to Silesia, and he was obliged to strew it with the bones of the most motley, ignorant, no, stupid soldiers. This made him very despondent.

Though constantly travelling the bumpy roads between his Rhine encampments and the Court at Vienna, he always found time to spend with his Italian ballet or French theatre and to promote either peace or intrigues between minor courts, princes, and towns by means of letters, gifts, threats, and troop manoeuvres, none of which he took the least bit seriously. He liked to compare nations to his women at Court. When a prince offered to be his ally, he would inform his retinue that he had entered into an affair with such and such a principality and that she was rouging her cheeks to make herself more presentable; when, at dinner or at cards, the subject of negotiations with Saxony came up, he would remark that Saxony was about to go into labour; and when his generals pointed to an inauspicious position on the right flank with possible repercussions in Westphalia, he would retort that poor Nassau would simply have to lose her virginity. Yet there were times when, looking out of his carriage at the misery and sickness of war-torn Bavaria, he would feel a sudden, inexplicable ennui.

Given that Charles placed states on the level of dancers and hard-headed actresses, he avoided conflict, and had avoided it that spring, after his contacts in Versailles informed him that Prussia was negotiating an alliance with the French and would attack before the year was out. But Vienna was impatient and kept ordering him to attack. Finally, towards the end of spring, he yielded and made ready to see the battlefields, corpses, burned-out streets, disembowelled women, rains, forests, mountains, and fields his soldiers would see, but all as if on a stage, without dirtying his hands, without losing his jaunty tone and courtly manner. He feared only that he would have the coarse, hot-tempered Count Bacciani – all ambition and blood lust – attached to him.

So when forced to cross the Rhine and, as he put it, play a round of faro with the French king, which he considered a stupid, futile provocation, he pictured the hostilities, amid the balls and banquets he gave before setting off, as a play put on by his theatre, a play whose cast would be made up not of troops but of a crowd of madmen and misfits with nothing better to do. He sent the men off slowly, his plan being to set up a vanguard in the hills and fields and let it fight as best it could, while he looked down from the heights, conserving his strength for the true enemy, who in far-off Silesia was conspiring to make life difficult for him.

It was for this reason that Field Marshal Lieutenant Johann-Leopold Bärenklau, the much feared conqueror of Bavaria and Charles's personal choice to lead the campaign, took up a position in the sparse woods on the right bank of the Rhine, downstream from Worms and Mainz. The troops consisted of Croatian, Hungarian, and Serbian cavalry regiments, a select border-guard infantry of pandours and haiduks, and an emergency reserve unit, called the Brigands, recruited from the woods of Slavonia by Count Trenk.

Charles had been forced to deploy this army; he did not care for it. It was poorly clothed, it stank, it was impossible to command. It was continually early or late, moved according to laws he was unable to ascertain, and caused unforeseen difficulties in general. It attacked when he did not wish it to and took flight when he least expected it to. It did not know how to shoot, it did not know how to manoeuvre. Its men kept getting sick or drunk, and plundered wherever they were quartered. Worst of all, it sustained such frightful losses that he could never use it in conjunction with more costly, better-trained troops, for fear of losing them as well.

Although Charles of Lorraine did not care for this army, Baron Bärenklau loved it dearly: these were the men with whom he had conquered Maria Theresa's rival Bavaria and had thus become her favourite. True, there were times when the wild, greasy, shaggy, mustachioed savages made him curse his calling, times when their frequent illness, carousing, and brawling made him lose his patience. Yet he always forgave them. He liked them. Besides, he did not need to bother about them, to feed or clothe them; they would sleep in the mud, ford any river, march until they dropped; they had no idea what they were fighting for, nor did they ask. Unlike Charles, he found them far from disobedient; indeed, whenever he set off on a campaign with them, he thought himself on a hunt with a loyal pack of hounds he could set on anything that came his way. If he was harsh, even merciless with them, it was because he trusted them to do miracles for him. Though he knew only a few words of their language, he could divine their thoughts. He tormented them all, men and officers alike, but made peace with them the next minute. He led them into the fiercest battles when they were exhausted, and put up with their drunken uproar afterwards. But he did not regard them as lecherous, plundering beasts; on the contrary, they struck him as retiring, reserved, almost melancholy. Most were well built but ungainly, not the type to put on parade. They made a great deal of trouble at inspections, yet he always saw to it that they were reassigned to him. For he, like all their officers, Isakovič included, knew that they were unsurpassed in combat. They fought like madmen. They slaughtered the enemy, grabbed him by the chest, flung him to the ground, tore his throat open, ripped his skin like ribbons, cracked his ribs with their guns, hands, and knees, smashed his skull as if it were a pumpkin. That was why when anyone at Court said to him, mockingly, "You and your pandours!" he would reply with great pride, "All mine."

Field Marshal Lieutenant Bärenklau's face was as wrinkled as that of an old priest and always pale. It was a face that never smiled, that bore the marks of all that he had seen – not behind the Slav warriors, but beside them, in the front lines, sword in hand. They had made him famous with their butchery, and he had stuck by them. He loved war at close quarters, and close quarters meant close to his men. He may not have been completely open with them, yet he treated them magnanimously, and rode silently at their side as they advanced or retreated. He was famous at Court for going months without music, salons, and a bed; but war was nothing to him if not endless carnage, cruelty, and suffering, all experienced face to face. He had lost all fear; he had come to believe he could win a battle merely by being present, and stopped heeding councils of war, briefings at headquarters, missives from the Court. To advance, all he needed was a rainstorm or a cloudy night. He preferred to attack after dark, setting off on the spur of the moment, in complete silence, after instructing the men to slaughter without mercy.

Skin and bones to begin with, he had grown even thinner from lack of sleep and nourishment. His cheeks were sunken, his Adam's apple bulged, his eyes glittered like a hermit's. His face – below a broad, furrow-riddled forehead and brows like canopies over large ice-blue eyes – lengthened from campaign to campaign; his mouth, buried in wrinkles, was as irregular as the sawlike teeth it housed. Though chronically hoarse, he shouted commands loudly and clearly, and the men, who called him the Old Crone, feared him as they would a witch. He had terrifying hands, all bone, and he wore either black silk and velvet with gold trim or armour and heavy hunting boots.

Such was the man awaiting Isaković on the Rhine, amid the sparse woods beyond Stockstadt, where he had deployed, inspected, drilled, and tormented the regiments led by Vuić, Horvat, and Wenzel and was dispatching spies nightly to the opposite bank, especially to Mainz.

Not only had Isaković failed to overtake the others; he was three days late. Bärenklau had had excellent reports on him from Ingolstadt, Graz, and especially Pécs, whose Governor had written an extremely long and detailed account in an ornate, spindly hand, praising the officers and their men, their arms and their reserves, but raising the issue of their Orthodoxy – they were schismatics, after all – and its bearing on their fealty to the Empress.

Though Baron Bärenklau had been brought up by Jesuits and therefore had a low opinion of the schismatic clergy in his army, he took the Governor's qualms with a grain of salt. It was an issue that could wait till the war's end; indeed, what was wanted now were additional monks, to help after the campaign and during the winter, when many of the men would be dying. He had noticed that the Serbs had a deep-seated need to sing unto the Lord and lament their dead, wailing and carousing, for nights on end by the fires in their camps.

Isakovič was bringing a crack regiment of three hundred men, whom he would use in a series of sieges, and Bärenklau had every intention of promoting him to lieutenant colonel if he survived. The plan for the sieges, a plan Charles of Lorraine considered his own, was now ready. It was to open with a surprise attack, from the flank, on Mainz, move up the Rhine to Worms and Speyer, then on to Fort Saint-Louis and Strasbourg, which would serve as a base for deep incursions into Lorraine, allowing Charles to invest the territory easily with his own massive troops.

When Isakovič did at last arrive, he spent the first night with his men in the woods overlooking Stockstadt, the Rhine, the tributary Bärenklau had chosen as his first objective, and rolling hills in the distance. The men stretched out in the warm, starry summer night, looking forward to a good night's sleep after days of uninterrupted marching. They almost felt they had come home: the same kind of grasslands, the same river, the same swamps, sand, willows, with blue hills in the background, storks soaring out of rushes, frogs croaking through the night.

But at the first rays of the sun a wizardlike Bärenklau rode past with the command that they immediately be woken and prepared for inspection at the foot of a nearby hill.

As in their homeland, the dawn creeping down the steep, dark hills to the luxuriant grass of the lowlands was magnificent. It reached the river in silence, like a breeze crossing the water's stagnant spiderweb surface of barely perceptible green dragonflies. Branches floated down the middle of the river, where the current was faster, but the opposite bank was still wrapped in haze. All that could be seen there among the dense thickets was a line of trenches and two French cannons.

Not far from the bank lay a dark island, also densely overgrown, which Bärenklau intended to link with his positions by means of a pontoon bridge. To do so he needed several men to dig a redoubt on the island by night, because the bank was all sand to the first trees and therefore afforded no protection from French bullets.

Isakovič's men looked out over the great empty space above the trees to the opposite bank, wondering what it contained. Not daring to descend to the water to wash, they smeared their belts, weapons, wheels, and aching feet with grease. Then, without the usual din, they formed into long lines and emerged from the wood half asleep, unsure of foot, bumping into one another and tripping over stumps in the semidarkness as they attached long bayonets to their rifles.

By the time day broke from behind the hills, the officers, whispering their commands – though they might as easily have shouted, so little chance was there of the enemy's hearing them – had got them to fall in near a patch of cut vines overrun by ground squirrels. While the men stood listening to the larks and staring at the strange roofs of Stockstadt, not daring to move lest the freshly greased barrels of their rifles should pick up dust, the officers inspected their packs, knives, and pistols. When Isakovič rode up at last, they stopped and stood at attention. He was wearing a brand-new bright red uniform and seemed ready to burst from under his hat. He too was closely shaven, having been scraped with a vengeance that morning by Arkadije, his orderly. Arkadije, who rode behind him, still half asleep and badly hung over, though less than steady on his own mount, was leading another horse, a white one, known to be cantankerous.

For a whole hour Isakovič rode up and down the ranks, forming them into two perfectly straight lines facing the flag. He forbade them to budge except to stretch a leg from time to time. They stood waiting for nearly four hours, though the inspection was to have taken place immediately. The sun was high in the sky, and still no Bärenklau. He had spent his morning riding along the bank listening for signs of action in the enemy's camp.

When at last he appeared, it was without warning, jiggling on his horse, accompanied by a group of officers and musketeers, and with hardly a nod at Isakovič. Isakovič had the men give a cheer for Maria Theresa, a salute to the flag, and a cheer for Bärenklau, which, despite repeated scoldings, came out "*Vivat* Ränbeklau!" Next he made them charge straight at Bärenklau's retinue, knives in teeth, which made even the generals uneasy but sent a shiver down Bärenklau's spine. He then put them through a variety of drills and ended with a volley of shots.

Field Marshal Lieutenant Baron Johann-Leopold Bärenklau, whose legs were so long they seemed to curl around his horse's neck, undertook to look the men over one by one, at the same time entertaining his companions with battle tales, a sign that he was in the best of moods. When he had finished, he told Isakovič to report to him at noon and asked, on his way to the flag, which he saluted, whether the men were good rowers. But just as he was about to leave, to Isakovič's great relief, he turned and frowned. Arkadije, who was supposed to keep out of sight, had suddenly lost control of the white horse and was swaying in his saddle in a manner impossible to ignore, especially against the background of the regiment, which was standing stock-still.

"What the devil is that man doing?" Bärenklau hissed, glaring at Arkadije. It was extremely important to him that the first review should proceed as majestically as possible.

Isakovič, for whom the success of the review was equally important, made no reply.

Seeing the frowning face before him, Arkadije began to jerk at the white horse, but the horse, accustomed to caresses and kind words from him, failed to respond. Suddenly he felt himself sliding from the saddle. He clutched at his horse's mane. He had been drunk the night before – as he was every night, thinking of the impending deaths of so many in the regiment – but now his hangover evaporated in panic. Bärenklau's remark frightened Arkadije out of his wits: he had ruined everything, it was a nightmare. Writhing, still trying desperately to remain in the saddle, he unwittingly wrenched the girth loose and seized the white horse's swishing tail in an attempt to regain his balance. Bärenklau flashed him another furious glance, not noticing that one of his iron spurs had entered the flesh above his ankle, and set off at a trot with his generals, officers, and musketeers in tow.

Because Arkadije was obliged to follow Isakovič, who was escorting the commander in chief, he too set off at a trot. Although his body was bathed in sweat and he could not tear his eyes from the hills and the willows, he somehow managed to pull himself upright. Then, imagining what Bärenklau had said in German, he turned in the direction of the German officers and vented his fury with a curse.

Suddenly, as Bärenklau's retinue was crossing from one hill to the next and as the far bank of the Rhine – glittering in the sunlight, with the silhouette of Worms in the background – came into sight, the French opened fire on them. They spurred their horses, all except Arkadije, who, though he clearly heard the bullets whistling past, was transfixed by the view.

With the next round of shots, however, he dismounted and tried to lead his horse, but it was rooted to the spot. Whispering to one horse and tugging at the other, he kept an eye on the French outposts. In the hope of saving the animals, he decided to return to the first hill, where the underbrush would provide great shelter. He made a dash for it, but was forced to take cover almost immediately when enemy bullets started raining down on him again. He marvelled that the enemy had sighted him. Turning in the direction of the outposts and with the same fury he had vented on the Germans, he cursed the French.

He died a few moments later, during his fourth attempt to rise and drag the horses out of the line of fire. His entrails spilling out, his hand clutching his belt, he fell with an excruciating "Oh my God! Oh my God!"

That night Bärenklau ordered the construction of the pontoon bridge to the island. Eleven soldiers died; seven were wounded.

Thus began the Rhine massacre of the Slavonian-Danubian Regiment, which did not know the why or wherefore of it.

7

They Wandered About Like Flies with No Heads;
They Ate, They Drank, They Slept Only to Advance at
Full Speed to Death, Press on to Nothingness, According
to the Will of and for the Benefit of Others

The Lorraine campaign, during which the noble Vuk Isakovič and his crack regiment of three hundred soldiers fought continually in the front lines, was over in a few weeks. Field Marshal Lieutenant Johann-Leopold Bärenklau, commander in chief of the advance guard, quickly captured the trenches around Mainz in a surprise attack, and the town surrendered. Charles of Lorraine then crossed the Rhine with his large army. Three days later, having exchanged no more than a few rounds with the French, they entered Worms and thence, during a violent rainstorm and without so much as a pistol shot, Speyer. After three days of rest they set up camp outside Saint-Louis, but after bombing the town for days to no avail, they were bombarded themselves; moreover, the French dammed the river until it overflowed, sweeping away carts, horses, and cannons and nearly drowning them all. Since they had failed to take the town by storm, they bypassed it, reaching Strasbourg at the same time as the French King. A truce was concluded, but hostilities resumed almost immediately. Then came word that they were to enter Alsace, and they attacked Saverne, suffering appalling losses in the town while Trenk and his Croat pandours ambushed, caught, and slaughtered large numbers of officers and men in the surrounding woods. When they tried to advance farther into enemy territory, however, they were repulsed and beat a quick retreat to the Rhine, which they crossed at the village of Deinheim, burning their bridges behind them. Charles of Lorraine then made haste to Bohemia, Prussia having in fact declared war. Isakovič's men, who had opened the campaign in the front lines, now found themselves in the rear. Tired and ailing, they made their way to Schärding, on the Danube, where they learned that they would be spending the winter in the Upper Palatinate and that many of their relatives and friends had died in the other war, in Bohemia, serving Prince Atanasije Raškovič, a colonel from Varadin.

The whole campaign was so senseless that Vuk Isakovič had the impression he had split in two: he was the Vuk who rode, shouted, shot, brandished his sword, forded rivers, and rushed into the fray at Mainz and Saint-Louis, but also the Vuk who walked like a shadow by his side, observing, silent. Ignorant of Bärenklau's intentions, he and his men lived from day to day. They spent nights in pouring rain, unsheltered, weeks without tents or a change of clothing. If his advice was sought, it was only at the last moment, immediately before a charge, and he was never told the name of the town under assault or where to proceed once the battle was over. Not knowing why, with whom, or for whom he was fighting, he began to plod on the battlefield, unconcerned with what was happening around him. When even after his victories he failed to achieve the rank of lieutenant colonel, he stopped shaving and trimming his nails, stopped caring for himself altogether, and when he was summoned before Charles of Lorraine at Strasbourg, he looked like a wild bear.

Gall rose in his throat and spread to the rest of his body; he could feel himself growing feeble, piece by piece, and wept for himself to himself. His bandy legs caused him endless pain on the battlefield, his feet swelled, his calves developed bumps, and the knee that had been kicked by the horse before he set out on the campaign had lost all flexibility. His belly sagged, as did his cheeks, and his eyes were bloodshot. He was completely grey now, long past the grizzled stage women liked so much, and his hair fell out and stuck between his fingers when he lifted his head from the bucket after his morning wash. His lips were blue, he had trouble breathing, his hands trembled, and he had resigned himself to stomach pains after every meal. When particularly dejected, he would stand in the field of white tents like a goose in a meadow and, legs spread wide, hands shading his eyes, stare up at the sky. Württemberg had left him so subdued that he exchanged only the briefest of words with his officers.

"I hereby vow," he had said to Captain Antonovič outside Saverne before sending him and several cavalrymen into town on a reconnaissance mission, "to feed the poor at my own expense, for the greater glory of our regiment and the honour of my name."

When the captain, seeing him so infirm, distressed, and dispirited, said, in the hope of cheering him, "I too feel moved to contribute to the greater glory of the Empress . . .," Isakovič, furious, interrupted. "Don't you see that the riches are vanity, vanity of vanities?" he shouted. "For even as all earthly goods perish, so shall all earthly glory. If I am near to death, the blame lies not with our ruler the Empress but in my ailing entrails. Now go." And he turned his back on him.

Whether or not Maria Theresa succeeded in placing her husband on the throne of Prussia once the war was won was as of little concern to Isakovič as his promotion was to her; he had no more feeling for Prussia than he had for Lorraine. If he thought about anything of the war he had been fighting, it was certainly not the towns, the state of their fortifications, or the deployment of the enemy's forces; it was the pointless tramping through hot, rainy summer nights, over hills, along riverbanks, and the acacias, and the changing skies and seasons. He had come all the way to the Rhine, through several foreign lands, as in a dream, acutely aware of the vain and fleeting nature of things. Yet he had rejoiced at the rumour that the next campaign would be against the Prussians, in Bohemia, in the vicinity of Cheb, because Raškovič had recently moved the remains of Prince Djuradj Brankovič from Cheb, where he had been tortured and, if regimental hearsay was to believed, poisoned.

His most pressing concern, however, was the regiment's rank and file, his anger and bitterness on their account eating away at him, all the more as he had no one to whom to unburden what he felt. The months of feverish anticipation of promotion had made him so miserable that he had grown insensitive to the misery of others – the rags the soldiers wore, the stench of the wounded who requested to stay with their comrades, the ease with which the men were packed off as cannon fodder. The entire Slavonian-Danubian Regiment had only one doctor allotted to it. And Lieutenant Colonel Vuič, who commanded two regiments, was constantly sending him officers to beg for money, because the army contractors robbed him blind. During a truce soldiers were hanged for stealing a head of cabbage. In the end, men and officers alike were overcome with great lassitude and staggered about in the wake of battles as if sleepwalking.

Although Isakovič could not keep subsequent battles straight, he well remembered the night they first crossed the Rhine. Bärenklau had spent three days with them in the woods above Stockstadt. He had suddenly appeared in the garb of a simple soldier and led the men in the dark, like animals, through the undergrowth, where they stumbled into mud-filled pits or toad-infested bogholes to the muffled guffaws of those behind them. When they reached the water's edge, Bärenklau lay with them in the sand under the foliage, listening for the French across the river.

The moon was full. They lay still, breathing on one another's mud-encrusted sandals and sharp knives. But they had a clear view of the murmuring river that flowed slowly past and the stumps and branches swept along by it. If a branch veered off in the direction of the other bank, the French would greet it with a round of shots. Otherwise the silence was so deep, they could hear dogs barking all the way off in Mainz.

All night they were covered with insects – the summer teemed with them – and the grass prickled their noses and ears. By morning their shirts were smeared with the juice of wild berries, their necks, cheeks, and hands with the slime of snails. Dawn found them wet and cold, caked with mire, listening to the woodpeckers in the trees. They could now make out the French soldiers in the trenches across the river.

From time to time during the next few days Bärenklau had them beat the drums or shout and light fires to make the French believe they were pitching camp. One night, when he felt he had sufficiently confounded the enemy, and the moon had begun to wane, he led his men down to the river again, this time closer to Mainz. Just before dawn he informed Isakovič of the plan of attack. Then he went off to find boats.

While the soldiers were asleep in a thicket, Isakovič crossed the sand to the river. He saw the starry sky, the woods on the opposite bank, two black islands in the middle of the water. Everything was quiet. He felt the dampness through his heavy riding boots, down to his toes. With a twist of his shoulders, weary yet pleasant, he freed himself of his greatcoat and felt how cold it still was. Lifting his pistol to the bridge of his nose, he again examined the powder charge, then engaged the safety catch. He drew his sabre, tossing the sheath over his shoulder in the direction of his men. Slowly, with as little motion as possible, he rolled his right sleeve up to the elbow and savoured the cold air on his hairy bare skin. His body was burning.

It was the greatest moment of his life. He felt that no one, nothing, could separate his fingers from the hilt of the sabre; he felt a swelling of his body sweeter than all ecstasy; he felt an end to all pain, a recovery so complete that he could hold back the river, pull out trees, cut down clouds.

He heard a soldier steal up to his greatcoat and grab it. Then he saw boats emerge from behind one of the islands. He went back to the men and led them swiftly out of the sparse woods along the bank to the point where Bärenklau was waiting for them with the boats.

No one said a word.

There were twelve large boats, each with a man at the oars. Bärenklau immediately jumped into the first one.

They pushed off the moment the boats were full, and soon reached one of the dark islands in the middle of the river.

Day was beginning to break; they could see no farther than fifty paces.

Skimming past the branches along the island's edge, they suddenly came out into open water and were sucked into a whirlpool. The first two boats grounded on sandbars. Isakovič saw Bärenklau stand and order the soldiers into the water to free the boats before they vanished in the semidarkness.

The remaining ten boats glided noiselessly on to the shore, and after hastily checking their powder flasks and fuses, the men disembarked, rifles in hand, knives in teeth.

The French were as yet unaware of their presence.

When Isakovič and several of his men appeared high on the bank, however, an enemy soldier let out a yell. At that very moment the two other boats touched shore and a rhythmic "Ma-ri-a The-re-sa!" rent the air. Then came a spurt of gunfire – the wild grunt of the enemy's artillery – and a terrifying roar: Isakovič's men had leaped into the trenches and started cracking heads.

Half an hour later Isakovič and a small advance contingent had made their way through the fallen, writhing wounded to the main street of the town. He was sweating profusely, gasping for breath, leaning with his blood-drenched sword on the walls of the houses. The soldiers around him shot at random into the dark, empty street. The two rows of pitch-black, pointed roofs nearly met, letting through only the narrowest streak of sky. And in it the morning star.

Thus it was that without any particular joy – or grief, for that matter – Vuk Isakovič gave safe passage to the delegation seeking Baron Bärenklau to surrender the town to him and hand over a cart loaded with corpses whose hands and legs still bounced with every bump. Nor did he derive any joy from the news that the main army was on its way and that the bridge had been completed. The three days it took for Charles of Lorraine's men to arrive he spent in deep, drunken sleep.

Two faces came to him in his dreams, two heads he had personally chopped off. They had left his memory, but hovered over his conscience for several days. Just as they were about to slip away completely, they made one last, momentary appearance – blurred, round, dripping blood, two halves of a pumpkin, the soldiers' main source of nourishment at the time.

Praised for his part in the Mainz venture, Isakovič remained at the head of the advance guard, in the mud at Worms. For every soldier his men killed he was given a silver florin by Charles of Lorraine. These he distributed to the men, along with an admonitory speech about the great Serb martyr Prince Lazar.

Several days later he was ordered to assist the army in laying siege to Fort Saint-Louis. His task was to attack the ramparts using saps specially dug for the purpose. It was one of the operations he had practised a great deal at home in Varadin.

The town of Saint-Louis lay on a verdant marsh. It was protected by the main course of the Rhine, a by-channel on the one side, and a system of ramparts and hidden moats on the other. Nights were impossibly muggy; mosquitoes were every-where. Days were quiet, with only an occasional hawk or flock of sparrows over the rushes. Had it not been for the cannons, Isakovič's men would have thought they were home.

They wailed all night to the sound of the gusla, leaning against the walls of their dugouts as earth trickled down their backs and dangling their legs in ponds as frogs hopped among the cattails. They sang because many had perished, many fallen ill. They mourned both the quick and the dead in chants so long and drawn out that while they sang, the enemy shot less and less, until the shooting stopped altogether.

In the meantime Isakovič had had a willowbranch and bulrush hut built for himself near one of the deep, newly dug saps. He managed to fit two cannons in it. It was so low that he had to crawl in on all fours, but when he lay on a flat bed of earth covered with a blanket, he could see nearly the whole town, its ramparts, and his own saps through the rushes.

There was a good deal to see. Whenever the shooting died down, his soldiers would roam about, distributing armfuls of cabbages, pumpkins and beans from ditch to ditch. When the French started bombarding them again, they scattered in all directions, falling into bogholes or sinking into quicksand like pigs into mire. Then everyone would run out of the trenches and after the cabbages.

For a few days all Isakovič did in the torpor he pereived as slow death was receive the emissaries Bärenklau dispatched to him with orders and reports. Though a first-rate leader, he had let up when he realized his promotion was not forthcoming. He had made not a single nocturnal raid or attacked even the closest trenches. Vuk Isakovič was tired of the war.

On the night the French dammed the by-channel and flooded his saps, drowning horses, sweeping away carts, and clogging cannons, he was sound asleep in his hut, dreaming he was marrying off a daughter with the exquisite face and figure of Princess Alexandra of Württemberg in the days of her youth. His favourite saint marched behind her in the procession: Holy Prince Stefan Štiljanović, the one in whose honour he and his brother, Arandjel, wished to consecrate the church they were building on the site of their father's grave. The Prince paused for a moment near him, gave him a beautiful smile, and said, "I see your last breath and the portal of your passing open wide. But first your wife shall be devoured by worms and the bitterness pass from your soul. And only when your long life has run its course shall your descendants see fair-eyed Dawn in the night."

Isakovič was sleeping so soundly, speaking between snores to saints and angels, that he woke only after his hut had capsized and he fell into the deep by-channel overflowing its banks into the plain around the fort.

The men spent all night keeping their heads above water, tramping through mud, digging out cannons. It was several days before the Austrian troops reassembled. This time they camped far from the town walls. Nor did they attack, but rather circumvented Saint-Louis and moved on to Strasbourg.

At Strasbourg Isakovič slept even more. The hussars rode straight up to his tents and shot their long rifles under his nose. But his men killed only small numbers of the French advance guard.

Every morning the tree-lined walls and trenches of the town floated before his eyes in a sea of sun-drenched grass. He would gaze up at the lofty steeples; he would gaze beyond them at the violet sky wet with rain, and below them at the rose windows, large and blue. It occurred to him that this would not be a bad place to live. One evening, when the cavalry brought him some prisoners, he interrogated them in great detail, through an interpreter, about their officers and system of ranks, especially colonels and lieutenant colonels. He was trembling with helpless rage.

Bärenklau, driven to despair by the manner in which Charles of Lorraine chose to wage the war, had pushed his advance guard to the town walls. Through Vuič he commanded Isakovič to storm a large stone watchtower whose gates remained open by day. One night, therefore, Isakovič roused his officers from their sleep and without much enthusiasm ordered them to wake the men, those who had not slipped out to plunder the local gardens for cabbages and melons. While the men crawled out of their tents, as hairy and unkempt as a herd of black rams, Isakovič pointed out the watchtower to the officers. In the boundless silence before daybreak it looked like a huge boulder. Through their spyglasses they could make out the sentries on the ramparts, a few roofs, and some green treetops. A milky mist hung over the meadows, reaching to the horses' knees. No one in Isakovič's camp suspected a thing. The guards, scattered among the tents, carts, and haystacks, stood leaning on their rifles like shepherds on their staffs, half asleep.

He rode out into the green fields and the empty, starry morning, warming himself with the steam that rose from his mount. Once he reached the wooded area from which he planned to launch the attack, he peered across the fields to the quiet trenches and the wall they would scale with blood-curdling cries before the sun was up. He turned to watch his men gathering around the officers and loading their rifles and pistols.

Jolting back to camp, his horse, startled for some reason, kept wrenching its head to one side. Isakovič felt a sudden renewed surge of the physical bliss that took hold of him before a battle and meant more to him than any other pleasure. As it ran through his body like a shiver, he spurred the horse and galloped the rest of the way, now eager to lead his men into battle. The horse's gait obliterated all his recent agony, his aching bones and joints, and a single deep breath of the grass, the dew, the warmth of the animal, the pungent metal odour of the arms overcame his nocturnal fevers, his wine-induced vapours, his spleen. Back in the camp, his horse frisking in circles, he let out such a whoop that the men drew back instinctively. He was about to scold them for sneaking out at night to pillage, to give them his usual short speech about death, perhaps bringing in Holy Prince Stefan Štiljanovič, when all of a sudden a French bugle blared in the distance.

The French King, it seems, had taken it into his head, while passing through the area, to visit besieged Strasbourg and pay his respects to the army. He happened to arrive on the day Vuk Isakovič, on Baron Bärenklau's orders, was preparing with his Slavonian-Danubian Regiment to storm a watchtower so poorly secured that its guards had not even bothered to dig themselves in.

Immediately following the bugle's call, French units began marching out of the town. They gathered on a field in front of the entrenchments, then set out, almost within shooting range of the Austrian camp, on the road that led past the tents of their advance guard, with the inhabitants of the town cheering and waving. While cavalrymen galloped ahead to catch an early glimpse of the young King and officers arrived from neighbouring garrisons, hundreds of musketeers and members of the King's bodyguard wended their way in and out of the double line of stationary troops. At last the King's carriage passed through. It was drawn by eight white horses and accompanied by a large escort of guards prancing on mounts, brandishing sabres and twisting this way and that as they strained to make out the Austrian advance guard in the distance.

The town fired a three-hundred-cannon salute, the army three salvos. Isakovič and his officers, lying in the shelter of a copse, observed the spectacle through their spyglasses and with their bare eyes, unable to do anything but await orders from Bärenklau.

Meanwhile, Charles of Lorraine had concluded a truce, and the Serbian camps immediately resounded with the scrape of the gusla, the wail of lamentations, and the stamp of the kolo. After a roll of drums, all the soldiers were warned against plundering during the truce, the penalty for stealing even the smallest fruit or vegetable being death. Whereupon the regiment sank again into great din and uproar, greasing legs, knives, guns, cartridges, and belts from dawn to dusk except for morning rifle drills and afternoon *vivats* on the parade ground, when the only Latin that came out right was the *vivat* itself; Carolus de Lotharingia, even after the thousandth time, became Calorus or Calodus de Lothragingia. As soon as it grew dark, guards and beatings notwithstanding, off the men would go to the surrounding villages, foraging for anything edible.

Isakovič thought he would go mad if the war went on thus any longer. Like Vuič, Markovič, and the other commanders, he spent most of the day cooling his heels at the quartermaster's tent, hoping to win his men a little more grain. He was mortified by his ragged tents and the wild dogs that had taken up residence in the few carts he had left – especially when he had constantly before his eyes the image of cattle grazing peaceably outside the town's walls and peasants shaking the last fruits of summer from the trees.

The next day, two of Vuič's men were hanged for stealing apples. An Austrian cavalry detachment that included a priest and a hangman happened to be patrolling the area and hanged them on the spot. The priest heard their confessions before their death.

Isakovič had a new hut built for himself. He ordered it dug into the ground and covered with grass, and he positioned the entrance in such a way that he could not see the town. What he saw was a camp littered with rotten straw and dogs howling and tossing it into the air with their muzzles. Still waiting for orders, he did not dare leave, though his officers freely visited other regiments, went hunting, frequented local taverns, and roamed the neighbouring villages in search of women.

By now he was not only certain he would not return from the campaign alive but also sorry he had put in for a promotion. It was clear that the days of the Turkish Wars were over, and that Charles of Lorraine gave not a fig for Isakovič's regiment, or Vuič's or Horvat's.

This alien land where he was fighting had worn him out and been the death of many of his men. The meeting with the decrepit Princess kept gnawing at his brain, and for days he had mourned his orderly, Arkadije, whose body and horses were never found. Some peasants must have run across them, fleeced the corpse of valuables, tossed it into the Rhine, and made off with the horses.

And now, he thought, he would die too. His heavy boots had lost their colour, his baggy trousers, which he patched himself, their shape. His face was copper from walking in the wind and sun, his body inured to hardship. Once more his belly made him look like a barrel, and he had aged greatly. Yet after a good day's sleep, and despite his sadness, he ogled the peasant girls. Thinking ahead to death had made him gentler, yet he still punched horses with his fist.

When he stopped shaving, his features acquired a calmer, gentler expression, but when a Catholic priest was attached to the regiment, his black-speckled yellowish eyes had a feverish sheen. He made a list of the men he wished to send home, and presenting it to Captain Antonovič, he spoke less like an officer than like a priest. "Read this with great care," he said, "and tell me whether I have sinned in matters of probity. Then write as follows: 'These men have traversed all Lorraine and fought gloriously. When they return to their homes, they are to remain in military service.'" He was sorry that he had to send them back to Varadin, that he could not, with one of his ornate signatures, send them on to Russia.

Lying in his lair, he came to the conclusion that he was as useless and ridiculous as a potbellied priest who kept giving sermons but had nothing new to say. As often happens at the onset of old age, he could see nothing before him but an abyss, a void.

When he set out to face death for the fourth time in his life, he had done so in the hope that something important would befall him; it had not. He had pictured himself and his men in a powerful army and glorious battles, basking in something that he could not quite identify but that was gratifying and significant, for him and for his men. He had left behind a number of concerns weighing heavily on him that spring: the quarrel with his brother over his wife's dowry, the illness that left his daughter covered with scabs, his wife's disconsolate outbursts, which he could no longer control, and above all the muddy village near Varadin, whose inhabitants were now putting up houses made of clay bricks and constantly begging for food, building materials, and a chance to serve in the army – though moving on to richer, more established villages when it suited them. After the difficulties he had experienced in the days before his departure – digging wells for drinking water and struggling with the church he was erecting in the middle of the village – he had been glad to leave.

The distress he felt over the destitution everywhere in the village – in his own house and sties and outbuildings and all the way along the river to Varadin – was augmented by the trouble he had had with Marquis Guadagni, commander of the Osijek fortress, while involved in the redistribution of the Slavonian peasant population and therefore in Patriarch Šakabenta's various solicitations and petitions. He came to feel the futility of the lives they were living, lives of migration, colonization, of lamenting the dead and bringing new people into the world, there along the Danube. He imagined escaping the vapours of the swamps and marshes, the endless day-to-day suffering caused by moving from place to place, watching cattle drown, ploughing through mud and bogs. One warm spring morning he would ride up a lofty hill and there be given something to save them all, make them happy. And he saw himself and his men returning from the war, riding down the other side of that hill, arriving home elated, finding everything different and full of joy. His wife and children would be safe with his brother, and someone was sure to take care of the villagers who had remained behind, and he would find them all healthy and reaping tall wheat, and he would be able to forget the thefts and murders he had had to deal with there on a daily basis. Hoping that the hand of God or of Caesar would protect his troops until then, he took great pains to see that the names of their villages and detachments were entered in a fine hand on the list the Governor was sending by special courier to the Council of War in Vienna.

While he was growing up, his father, who sold cattle to the Prince of Savoy, had made all his children and relatives – his entire family, everyone he knew – join the Austrian army, which was fighting the Turks at the time, and in his youth Vuk had made a fine life for himself there. Spoiled by his superiors and quickly promoted, he developed a deep-rooted feeling of joy and pride in the army, especially as he believed that the wars would eventually end in universal peace, which he and his relatives and friends and all his men would celebrate by donning special festive uniforms and circling the battlefields, circling the Empire, greeted everywhere by shouts of "Here come the Serbs!"

Under the influence of his father's repeated assurances that Serbia would revive, no matter how devastated or desolate it became, he had enjoyed serving in the army in peacetime and during all three wars. Not until after his father's death, when he started sinking ever deeper into the side of military life that included colonization, census-taking, and rounding up men and livestock from various fortresses and military villages, did he realize that things would not improve. Not until then did he notice the bogs and marshes around him, the poverty of his men, the bleak, day-in, day-out monotony of their lives both in the trenches and in their huts and dugouts.

More recently he had been discouraged by the humiliations he had suffered at the hands of his superiors, both in military affairs and in his dealings with the Patriarch. This war, beginning with Pécs, had failed to bring relief; indeed, by the time he crossed the Rhine, he felt he had been intentionally humiliated. He saw his actions as if they were someone else's; he walked among corpses through burnt-out villages as if in a dream. And now, during the wretched truce outside Strasbourg, he felt a terrifying, dizzying chasm before him, a void.

Lying for days on a horse blanket in stifling heat under the low roof of intoxicatingly fragrant dry grass, with a jug of water and virtually no visitors, he moved only to turn from the beating sun to the shade and to brush away the ants that gathered under his saddle pillow. With his stomach, which bothered him less since the fighting had begun, he lay still, as in a tomb, and put off inspecting the camp from one day to the next. It had turned into a real Gypsy camp, the men wailing to the gusla around the fire more out of hunger than from drink. Whenever he stretched his arms and legs, half asleep, he imagined that they reached all the way to Bärenklau's tents, that he could tumble the town walls with his feet and strangle any number of Bärenklaus with his hands. In his impotent fury he drifted off several times during the day, to be awakened at dusk by soldiers singing and drums beating.

His face puffy with sleep, his body bloated, again, he leaned out and listened – through the camp's din and the clump of hooves, through cow bells and anvil hammers – to the relentless chirp of crickets in the fields. He leaned out and stared into nothingness, the void that had opened before him and his old age. He did not ask for his officers, afraid they would impose their worries and their feasts on him; nor did he venture to Bärenklau's tent, where there was always a card game and great merriment.

All alone – a few carts hung with assorted gear and the

endless scorched fields and burning sky his only perspective – he lost all hope: he gave up on his promotion and on Baron Bärenklau, whom he had admired at first. Not only did the army – for which he and his men opened the way by slaughtering and being slaughtered – seem inconsequential, but his past too, which he now saw as pure folly. Nor had he any hope for the settlers he had moved into his village, pitiful, cheated creatures that they were.

The thoughts leading him to despise and abandon the army and the settlers inevitably led him to similar thoughts about the rest of his life: his wife and daughters, who had caused him such torment and who were not here to see him, touch him, comfort him.

That evening, lying in the hut, he saw his life disappearing into the void. It was gone; he threw it off the way he threw off his silver-braided uniform when he was with a woman, to make her laugh. That evening, in his dreams, a hag came to him in place of his first love, the void in place of the towns where he had lived and traded and killed.

The only specks of light in his memory now were pure, radiant stars and woodland paths with a silvery April mist upon them, like the stars he had seen and the paths he had ridden with his wife in the first weeks of their marriage, when they lived a monotonous provincial garrison life, chasing foxes and dreaming of boundless, snow-swept Russia, to which he longed to migrate and live a better life, a life in which he would at last know peace.

As Isaković left the hut that evening, his mind and soul were on matters other than the wounded on their straw pallets, the hobbled horses, the tents, the guns, the powder kegs, the guards who greeted him. He gazed out over the sunken camp paths that seethed with men and heat, then at the horizon. There was no end to the unbearable swelter, not a cloud in the sky, and the mountains rising in the distance, the scorched grass, even the fruit trees smelled of dust and heat. He saw trees and bushes lining the river as if on a pilgrimage to the spires of far-off village churches; he saw huge haystacks on the slopes beyond the fortifications, a motley mosaic of burned and harvested fields; he saw the orchards, where the French had dug in their cannons, rising on hillocks out of endless marshy lowlands. The town, quivering in the heat, seemed suspended in air, the roads around it dark with carts and cavalry, like banks of clouds.

He was sitting with his back against the hut, not yet in full uniform, when Captain Antonovič, who was on night duty, came and read his report and an invitation from Bärenklau to lunch the next day. Isakovič stretched his legs, broke a branch from a plant whose dry berries, crackling in dry pods, had brushed his face. Then he stretched out full length under the bush that sheltered his hut, closely watching the shafts of light that hovered in the distance over the trenches, and opened his shirt to the waist. He dismissed Antonovič with a gruff order not to arrest men leaving camp that evening or to report them to the guards when they returned in the morning.

Breathing in the scent of the burnt grass between the tents, he waited for night. Dusk descended slowly on the fields, accompanied by the barking of dogs. The first fires, on the far side of the trenches, lit up the faces of soldiers squatting by cauldrons as they peeled and sliced potatoes and pumpkins. A pale sky had crept down among the fruit trees, and cool air immediately followed. The wailing and the gusla started up again – this time with a fife and a Jew's harp – but soon the silence of night succeeded dusk and the camp disappeared behind a mist of darkness, its dust covering everything but the tops of the fruit trees. Now Isakovič felt calm.

Everything before him was nothingness and a void; everything behind him vanity. Yet he could not accept that it would all come to nought; an inner voice promised him that in the end something beyond the ordinary would happen.

He had reached the brink of an abyss, a bottomless pit; he

realized his life was over and he could not set it right, nor could he set right the lives of the men who had followed him and would perish here or return to the marshes, always dependent, always under orders. He had abandoned all hope, yet he still felt something above him, something like the sky that had cooled the summer evening.

Gazing across the broad, empty fields to the river and beyond, to the hills and sky, Isakovič felt that he had been born for something other than the sad, tedious void he found here far from home. Somewhere – as in that sheaf of light in the fruit trees above or in the deep dark of roofs filled with doves and swallows – somewhere there was a corner of heaven for him. A tranquil life, serenity, days that flowed like a pure, cool, frothy waterfall – it had to exist somewhere for him and his men. Lying there and sweating while his dogs panted and snapped at flies, he thought of a place as clean and clear and smooth as the surface of a mountain lake. He wanted to leave and take them all with him, the Patriarch as well, take them away from the mud, the endless wars, the service and obligations, take them away to live as they pleased, free from this frightful discord, free to lead their own lives, the lives they were born to, and search for something beyond the ordinary, something that like the heavens would cover and culminate all else. His former life, then, would not seem so pointless and vain, nor would his future be a void.

Never in all the weeks of strain and marching had he felt as he felt that night, leaning over the terrifying well of despair. It was a thirst for something joyful and radiant, something that would ensure he did not leave this world a miserable, empty wreck of a man. Never had the Honourable Vuk Isakovič so felt the need to hear a whisper from the starry heavens, a whisper that would tell him of his mission to lead his regiment, which now seemed to him more valiant than all others, more precious than anything on earth.

It was something beyond earthly concerns that Vuk Isakovič thirsted for on that sweltering summer night outside Strasbourg, and things not only for himself but for his men as well. Because he felt, humiliated and deceived, that he had been born for something pure, radiant, beyond the ordinary, and permanent, like the silver and blue patches of sky that hung all night below the brilliant constellations and above the roofs of the town, the grass, the hills, and the streams lined with the campfires of an army on which moonlight fell like a fine summer rain.

Immediately upon wakening, Isakovič learned that three more men had been caught and hanged for stealing. In a poorly worded report, Captain Antonovič emphasized that the officer responsible for the action, the head of a dragoon company, was a drunken cuirassier, a veritable beast known for pummelling men on the nose with the hilt of his sabre and hanging them without even giving them a chance to speak. To make matters worse, the company's Catholic chaplain had insisted on confession, so these Orthodox men, not allowed to pray to their God or send a message to their far-off loved ones, wept as they were strung up. After the men had been hanging for three hours, Captain Antonovič requested that they be given to Lieutenant Colonel Arsenije Vuič for burial, since at the last moment they appeared to have denied belonging to the Slavonian-Danubian Regiment.

Livid with rage and resentment, Isakovič plunged his head into the bucket of water he kept in front of the hut. He could feel his heart pounding as the water dripped down his naked chest. He ordered Antonovič to send two of their own monks to stay with the bodies, to go himself to Bärenklau, and to inform the regiment that no one was to leave camp without a knife. As he dressed, he gazed at the roads covered with French carts, at the dust, the larks skimming low over the fields, and the guards and trenches and ramparts. Suddenly his eye was drawn to a row of acacias and fruit trees marking the entrance to a village on the horizon, and he thought, yes, that was where the men were hanging.

While his horse was being harnessed, he stared, dejected, at the open fields. A grey murky sky spread over the teasel and thistle. There would be rain.

His horse stood snorting in the weeds and, though normally calm, shied when he went up to it, and as the men tried to tighten the girth, it began turning in a circle, fixing Isakovič with its large black eyes. He gave it a punch, and it shuddered and stood stock-still while he mounted. He set off with the thought that he could still ride like a young man, and tightened his belt a notch as he jolted over the fields.

Trotting into the hot, muggy gloom of the morning, past Bärenklau's herd of horses, past tall piles of shafts and wheels, past sacks, haystacks, and dug-in cannons, over broken fences, and through orchards full of felled trees, he kept his eyes trained on the acacias and houses at the horizon of the great green expanse before him. They seemed to move no closer, perhaps because his horse, snorting furiously at the nettles and bumps, stumbling, and knocking one hoof against the other, was giving him such a trouncing.

By the time he arrived, he was dripping with sweat. From afar he had spotted plots of pumpkins and tall hemp growing beside a stagnant pond, a cluster of houses, and cows grazing on an unmown meadow speckled with wild poppies. Near a tall haystack a group of peasants and their children and poultry had gathered around a cart with two large wheels, where two dragoons held their horses by the reins, looking very satisfied with themselves. From the flurry of motion, the bearing of the women and girls, the way in which the men stretched out their legs, and wiped their necks, Isakovič concluded they had been dancing.

Just before they noticed him, he jumped over a ditch behind the houses and hemp and made his way through a tumbledown gate to the other side of the pumpkins, where eight acacia trees edged the stagnant water. Several drops of rain fell on his face as he pulled in the horse. He heard a magpie overhead, then some crows.

The horse gave a great shudder, moved back a few steps, and stood still, its legs quivering.

The first thing Isakovič saw on the other side of the hemp were two larks hopping through the stubble of a field that ended in a hill blocking the view of a good deal of the town. Following the horse's tug to the right, he saw the orchard bordering the pumpkin patch and three scarecrows peacefully swinging back and forth from three pear trees. They had been strung so low that they nearly brushed the pumpkins, whose large yellow flowers hid long ripe cucumbers. As their knees had not been bound, their legs, in tight grey trousers, dangled; they might have been sitting on high stools. Their bare feet were swollen and blue, as if frostbitten. Seeing them hanging like so many skinned sheep kept him from raising his eyes.

When at last he did, he saw that the men's hands were tied behind their backs and that their heads had not been covered. Their eyes and noses were teeming with flies, their heads twisted about, as though they had jumped wildly, with branches on their backs, above the ditch filled with stagnant water. On the far side of the pond, sparrows fluttered from haystack to haystack.

The tree from which the man closest to him hung still had quite a few ripe pears on it. Although his horse refused to move any closer, Isakovič could to his horror see the man quite well. He was short and rotund and appeared to have put up resistance: his shirt was in shreds and coming out of his trousers, which were torn at the knees. His head, a mess of hair, hung to the left, his throat bloated and covered with blood down to the rope, on which his blue tongue rested.

The man in the middle was a giant with long moustaches. One of his legs was crossed over the other, which touched the ground. The branch on which he hung must have cracked in the death agony, and the pears had fallen to the ground. During his shoulders' awful battle with the noose his lower jaw had sunk its huge yellow teeth into the upper lip, which was all blood. His head drooped back, its blank eyes staring at the blue sky.

As only the third man's neck had actually broken, he was the only one to hang straight, and his head lay so low on his chest that only its bloodstained grey whiskers were visible.

Not until they had hung for three hours did the dragoons take them down, in the pouring rain, and exhibit them in carts in front of the houses where they had been apprehended. On Isakovič's orders the monks he had had sent from Vuič's regiment performed the funeral ceremony.

He returned to his hut to find it full of water, and spent the night shivering under a cart in the utter quiet of the rain-drenched camp. Even the dogs were silent.

No sooner had he woken the next morning than he was informed that two of his men were lying black and blue at the main lookout and that a third, a veteran of the Turkish Wars who had been caught with a head of cabbage in his kerchief – for which he claimed to have paid – had resisted the dragoons with a knife and escaped.

Before the morning was over, Isakovič had had an audience with the general in charge, and before evening he was ushered in to see Charles of Lorraine himself, who feared that the runaway would go over to the enemy. While he spoke, he peered in amazement through his lorgnette at the wild, bearded Isakovič.

From that day on there were no more hangings. Men caught stealing were merely administered an impromptu bastinado. The runaway showed up that same evening, and, far from being reprimanded, he was rewarded with five ducats when he showed Charles his body covered with the scars from Turk-inflicted wounds.

Two days later French hussars broke the truce, and the Slavonian regiments set off for Saverne, where Bärenklau had in mind an ambush by which Trenk's and Markovič's cavalry would so massacre the garrison that even the general staff would surrender.

On the morning of the attack Isakovič awoke, tired, in a fold full of sheep, within firing distance of the town. The Austrian spy who was his guide had taken him under cover as far as the French outposts. Hidden by high grass, the Slavonian-Danubian Regiment once more found time to fill their stomachs before crawling through fruit trees up a hill that give them their first view of the town's roofs. They were so close that the sun reflected in the windows temporarily blinded them. Their tall black hats looked like a herd of black sheep emerging from the grass. The French sighted them immediately and opened fire, whereupon shots rang out from bushes and bosks on all sides.

In no particular order Isakovič's men hurtled down the hill toward the town gates and the first houses, which their cannonballs had set on fire. The town was quiet, dead except for the flames. On their way to the upper town and the fortifications, they saw infantry and artillery mixed together in a cloud of dust, moving on. Vuič's troops, which had entered the town from the west, were firing at the enemy in two ranks – one kneeling, the other standing – from a thicket, and each time the officer in charge shouted a command from his horse, they would shout it back with such force that individual words echoed over the hills and through the trees, all the way to the other side of town, which was sunny and still peaceful.

Isakovič, having stumbled down a steep, newly mown incline, came out on the road leading into town with several orderlies. A group of hussars was milling about the flaming remnants of a sentry box. The minute they saw him, they spurred their horses and galloped off. Isakovič ran after them, but they disappeared among the burning houses, and he found himself in a broad, empty street where all the windows were boarded shut. He turned back to see Bärenklau's carriage coming down the same path he himself had just taken, and the Field Marshal Lieutenant himself – dressed as a foot soldier but surrounded by officers – stepping swiftly beside his horse and waving at him, calling out something to him.

Isakovič's men swept into the town, filling the street with their shouting and stamping. He turned for an instant, saw the trees, the road from the valley, the approaching artillery, and soldiers flocking in on both sides. He looked up at the roofs and windows lined with flowerpots and down at his dogs barking furiously in the middle of the street as the horses passed. One of the servants leading them suddenly dropped to the cobblestones, hit by a stray bullet.

Ducking between the houses and turning back to the battle, Isakovič could not make out what Bärenklau was shouting. In the distance he saw his own soldiers falling, leaping up, pressing against the rows of houses. Only then did he realize that men were falling around him as well: salvos of French fire were thundering in his face.

In their retreat the French were trying to reach the upper town, the fortifications, from which they could make a run for the woods and safety. Little did they know that Trenk and his Croat pandours and Slavonian "brigands" were lying in wait for them. Crowded together, they fired one salvo after another, and the wide cobblestoned roadway, the side streets, and the house entrances were soon littered with corpses and black tricorns.

Hugging the smoke-covered walls, Isakovič led his dogs, bewildered by the smell of gunpowder, through the hell of horses that no longer flinched at the shooting and corpses. He could not find his regiment; the men had merged in the melee. When despite the terrifying confusion he finally realized that much of the shooting was coming from behind the boarded windows and bolted doors, he took refuge under an arch surmounted by a large blue wooden rooster. He stood there for several minutes between life and death, which were madly, ludicrously, incomprehensibly close to each other: he could just as easily be in this world, with its high grass, green hills – in this street, where the dead lay like brightly coloured dolls and the wounded screamed in pain – as in the other world, in peace, where the dead had now gone.

When bullets started striking the wall just above his head, he huddled lower and discarded all his weapons but his sabre. Suddenly two enemy soldiers appeared around the corner, only steps from him. Before they could get their bearings, however, Isakovič's orderlies had filled them with so many bullets and knife wounds that they barely had time to gurgle.

Meanwhile several of his men, having spotted him at last, came running up and, bent over to avoid being shot, enumerated the dead. The smoke was so thick that they could scarcely make out soldiers firing volleys no more than ten steps away. But when Baron Bärenklau's large carriage loomed into view, bumping over cobblestones torn loose by cannonballs, Isakovič ordered his men to open fire on the houses, both windows and doors. Then he threw off his hat, prodded his dogs, and tore into the middle of the street, brandishing his sabre and dashing from soldier to soldier, each of whom began a fresh assault the moment he recognized his commander. Isakovič gathered the men kneeling on the cobblestones, firing salvos into the smoke, and shouted, "Fire one! Fire two!" To the veterans waiting for the recruits to load their rifles he cried out, "Fellow Serbs, for Count Wallis! For Count Wallis, fellow Serbs!" Still brandishing his sabre, he turned now and then, hoping that if the enemy hit him, it would not be in the back.

Thus did the Slavonian-Danubian Regiment lose great numbers of its men before dark that evening in the hilly streets of Saverne, while pushing the enemy into Trenk's ambush, where the enemy too lost great numbers.

For the next six days Baron Bärenklau took up residence in the finest house on the main square, sleeping again in a bed and a long silk nightshirt. During the first two of those days the Slavonian-Danubian Regiment buried its dead, many officers among them, in trenches outside the town.

The taking of Saverne opened the gates of Alsace, but it proved the regiment's final battle in this campaign. After six days Charles of Lorraine recalled his troops en masse to the Rhine, which they crossed at the village of Deinheim on bridges in flames.

Isakovič's men, who had been the first to enter the town, were now the last to make their way out across the charred beams. All they left behind on the far side of the Rhine was dust and smoke, which dissipated quickly.

What happened subsequently was quite dismal. Hunger, thirst, marching, marching without end, marching through Bavaria – enemy Bavaria, plundered and bare – and on to Bohemia.

Autumn came earlier than usual, and the rains were heavy. Isakovič slept under his cart, racked with pain and anxiety. Having received no news of his brother or his wife, he had almost forgotten them.

Word reached the regiment that it would be quartered for the winter in the Upper Palatinate and that the other Slav regiments were already fighting the Prussians. There was also talk about their being sent home and then dispersed among the Emperor's regular units. To make matters worse, two Austrian officers were attached to the regiment. Within a fortnight Captain Piščević was thrown in chains and hauled off to be court-martialled for allegedly fomenting revolt. Charles of Lorraine had gone to Vienna, leaving Bacciani in command.

The Slavonian-Danubian Regiment set up camp on the

banks of the Inn near the town of Schärding and vanished into the autumn mists. Here too Isakovič slept, slept all day under his cart.

One day he heard that someone was asking for him in town, a merchant with news of his brother from Demitrios Kopsha, a Vienna merchant. He went down to the river that evening and waited at the ferry dock for the man, to whom he had sent word with a soldier. Because it was cold and stormy, he took shelter in a boat that had run aground in the underbrush at the foot of the steep riverbank. He could scarcely make out the ferry when it pushed away from the opposite shore.

Darkness was seeping into the mire, rain whipping across the horizon. When at last the ferry came near, he jumped up and ran down to the water's edge, calling out impatiently to the soldier he had sent to town and then, in German, to the merchant.

A corpulent man in a military greatcoat stood and called back that he had news from his brother, then, after Isakovič ran out into the mud, that he had news about his wife. Isakovič watched as the boat, large and black, pulled closer to shore, and after the final strokes of the oars he reached out and grabbed it, hauled it in with his hands. The man in the greatcoat, whom the soldier helped to step out, introduced himself as Joachim Riegel, a Schärding merchant, and said that three weeks earlier he had been in Vienna, where his friend and fellow tradesman Demitrios Kopsha had asked him to locate Vuk Isakovič – who was in the army and had failed to answer all letters addressed to him – and tell him that his daughters and brother were well but that his wife, Dafina, had died.

8

Tormented by the Void in Her Womb,
She Realized Her Soul Would Leave No Trace,
Not Even in Her Children, and She Regretted
Having Failed to Satisfy at Least Her Body,
Newly Awakened to Pleasure

Dame Dafina's appointed hour came on a hot day late in August, after a three-week drought. The bleeding from her womb, perhaps as a result of the Turkish healer's baths or the Osijek physician's metal tubes, had begun anew, and her blood gave off a frightful stench. All the women servants flocked around her, crossing themselves and casting spells.

The night before her death she had a high fever. She begged her brother-in-law to go and see the Patriarch and plead with him to have her admitted to a monastery, where she might still recover. She did not calm down until dawn, when she heard the menservants splashing buckets of water over Arandjel Isakovič's coach and leading out his horses. He had in fact been planning to visit the Patriarch: after many weeks of hesitation, he had made up his mind to talk to him and the other priests about the holy sacrament of marriage and the marriage of his brother, a marriage he had once contracted and now destroyed.

But Dafina saw and heard no more of the last dawn in her life. Exhausted by the fever, she fell into a deep, almost death-like sleep, her eyes sunken in their sockets, her skin showing every bone, every vein. Large beads of cold sweat trickled like dew down her eyelids. The pale light of day brushed her motionless features, her bluish lips and nostrils, with the same mute insensibility with which it brushed the tile stove beside her bed, the chair and cushions near her window, and the door, outlined in the semidarkness by a thin band of brighter light.

She no longer saw objects changing colour or the sharpening shadows cast by the window grille behind the curtain she had grown accustomed to seeing every morning, or the huge flies she had also observed in her illness when awake, flies gliding across the whitewashed ceiling with a quiet buzz that gained in intensity as they reached a wall and paused. Nor did she hear the river flowing past the house – a sound that disturbed her at first but later soothed her – or the water mill, distant but always audible.

She did not see the sun breaking over the hills, through the willows and thickets and swamps, or the storks and lapwings soaring over them, or the peaceful herds of sheep along the banks, which she used to follow, the sheep upside down in the water. Nor had she waked by the time the silver slip of the moon disappeared from the sky. Terrified as she was by her condition in the past few days, she had rejoiced to find it still in the deep blue outside her window. She did not see the long row of trees on the hill that appeared only after the sun flooded the surrounding plains, a sight she had come to know well in the past two months, each day awaiting that hour, for it was then that the marsh and mud below her window ceased their noxious emanations and the sun shone its light upon her, huddled in her chair, and illuminated her body from feet to waist in so agreeable a manner that it gave her hope she would recover.

She did not wake when the rest of the house woke around her – the bargees, shepherds, swineherds – or hear the squeaks of the well sweep, the grunts at the trough, or when her servants, having pushed the door open a crack, peeked in and, seeing she was asleep, tiptoed to the chest in which she stored her dresses, because in the last few days she had taken to sewing and they brought new material to her. Nor did she wake, her lips trembling and frothy, her teeth chattering, to the febrile images she often saw before dawn: the marshes and swampland her husband crossed as he rode up to her, his body mutilated, his belly slashed, eyes drained, skull cracked, arms open wide to hug and crush her, though she backed away like a shadow; columns of soldiers marching all around her, faster and faster; her husband's gigantic head, gruesome and bloody; far-off towns, where she ran breathless with her husband up steep streets while the two of them – but particularly she – were shot at by soldiers – no, not soldiers, weapons hanging in the air or on trees; and her brother-in-law, Arandjel, kissing her under the arm and tickling her, of which she had dreamed often and with pleasure during her illness.

From swoon to swoon she severed all contact with heaven and earth, lying motionless in her bed, bathed in sweat, dark as a corpse.

Yet shortly before noon she took a turn for the better. Looking around with large, tired eyes, she saw the thick white-washed beam engraved with the four letters of Christ's name. Her consciousness restored, she recognized her room, which was hung with sheets soaked in vinegar, and the two servants constantly tending her, dabbing her mouth and eyes while puckering their lips and crossing themselves. To her horror Dafina understood she was dying.

Her body writhing under the covers, her head rolling among the pillows, she tried to jump up and scream, but the servants held her, and her voice, which she thought loud enough to have crossed the river, barely reached the court-yard. She felt so much weaker than she had the day before that she burst into tears. The servants soon followed suit. Propped up on the pillows and mumbling, with a crazed look in her eyes, she seemed to be trying to catch something with her hand, and did not grow calm until her daughters were brought in. She was conscious, yet she often forgot where she was. For a while her eyes would close, only to fly open again; she would lose her hearing, then catch the merest whisper, stammer, and enunciate her words softly but with perfect clarity. Finally she fell into an agony that lasted until night.

Though perfectly aware that Vuk Isakovič was away, knowing even where he had gone, she desperately longed to see him. For years she had feared for his life, feared he would fall in battle, and she had grown accustomed to thinking – especially as he too often spoke of it – that he would return home covered with blood. She found it inconceivable that she should die before him, and even more so, that he should be absent when she died. She even wondered whether his presence might not have kept her from dying; in any case, it would have made dying easier, more like falling asleep. It never occurred to her that her infidelity might come between them; indeed, she had thought to tell him about it, along with the other trials she had endured during his absence. All that really mattered was that he be there, by her side, and she was certain that had he known she was dying, he would have come.

Four times that afternoon she thought he had entered her room, four times she asked for him, spoke of him as if he were present, until the servants, especially the old man Ananije, were convinced that the devil was making the rounds.

But her desire to see her husband was not so all-consuming that it excluded the desire – a desire every bit as strong, in fact – to see her brother-in-law, whom she kept expecting and asking for, whose step and voice she longed to hear that whole dreadful day. She no longer thought of him as repulsive and sallow; he seemed made of amber, especially when he gathered her knees into his impatient arms. True, her life with Vuk Isakovič kept coming back to her, but so hazily that she had difficulty picturing him whole. Her life with Arandjel Isakovič, which had begun so disagreeably on the night he first laid hands on her, seemed more real, the life of the future, a wonderful life, wonderful because now she would know she was alive in a way she had not thought possible.

Undecided on her deathbed, she realized she had been undecided all her life. She suddenly thought of the women (one was Turkish, the other two Romanian sisters, for whom she had never really cared) visiting her almost daily of late and telling her of their exploits with men. Now she saw how right they were to do what they did: at least they knew what they were living for. She envied them their dissolute, flamboyant existence, and in her feverish brain pieced together lascivious scenes from their lives. Recalling her brother-in-law's love games, she tried to convince herself, on this the last day of her life, that she had started a new life with him, a life of heady pleasures that made her former existence look miserable, worthless, appallingly worthless – from childhood with a step-father to maidenhood with an aunt, to marriage, children, and the uncertainties of a mindless, monotonous existence of poverty and migration.

As her breath came with greater effort, she went back over the emptiness of her life as a woman, which, like wheat tossed into the attic or dresses into her trunk, was divided between her husband and brother-in-law, their whims all but driving her mad. She had her servants bring her a mirror, the very same wrought-iron flower-framed mirror they had placed under her nose only hours before to see if she was still breathing. At the sight of her wrinkled brow, hollow sockets, and scrawny neck she knew how ugly the rest of her immobile body looked, and again burst into tears. While the two men went on living, enjoying life – growing old perhaps, yet free of the infirmity festering in her womb, free of the bleeding – she would be tossed out of the house like a rag.

Suddenly she noticed her daughters behind one of the sheets stretched across the room. She turned away from the younger girl, more out of disgust than pity, at the sight of her scabs, and concentrated on the elder, who, clutching the hand of a servant, was asking questions. She realized that even the elder daughter would retain only a dim memory of her mother. While pondering whether to marry the rich Arandjel, especially in the event of her husband's death, she had forgotten she had children. So tedious did she find them that she could not bring herself to ask after them, much less look after them. Now that she knew she was dying, she had the same feeling of helplessness about them as about all else she had been given and then deprived of. Everything was leaving her body, and leaving nothing behind – no gratitude, no future. All she had left now was an empty womb, a stench, and agony.

In the afternoon she was feverish again and regained consciousness at shorter and shorter intervals. Strange spirits, illuminated by the votive candle, kept approaching her bed. In fact, it was half of Zemun filing in to catch a glimpse of her.

At about five o'clock she awoke thinking of the horses Arandjel had given her, and ordered in a feeble voice that some sugar be taken to them. She also spoke of Arandjel in highly flattering terms and announced that she planned to move with him to Buda.

Shortly thereafter she opened her large, winter-sky-blue eyes again and, fully conscious, looked around the room with great serenity. She inquired about her husband and at the same instant recalled the early days of their marriage. Again she felt that the first summer was the only real time she had had with him – the grass, the leaves, the tiny flies and ants, and nights in the silver woods. When she thought of that marvellous time with Vuk Isakovič, Arandjel and his lovemaking seemed ludicrous. She pictured the garish blue, yellow, and green silks to which she was so partial, her fine, strong legs and straight shoulders, and a wave of self-pity came over her: she still thirsted for love.

She failed to notice the sun going down, or the heat, or the dust; she no longer knew where the hills were or the willows or the islands; she could not hear the water flowing past or the Greek prayers the priest at the far side of the room was mumbling.

At about seven she had the servants draw open the curtains and let in the summer-evening air. By then the noise of the barges, the sheep, the caravans of pack mules and their bells had died down. From the sweat-drenched head of her bed she watched the evening come as through a haze. Summoning her last strength, she asked the tearful servants to wash her, but then, to their great surprise, she started arranging her hair and ordered that her nails be polished. That done, she spread a carefully selected kerchief over her head and presented the pouch of ducats she kept under her pillow to Ananije, her brother-in-law's oldest retainer. Then she looked at the door as if waiting for someone to enter.

There she lay, washed and combed, her eyes wide open. No one dared approach her, not knowing whether she was dead or alive.

While his sister-in-law lay dying, Arandjel Isakovič jolted along in his coach, certain she would die.

The doctors had long since told him there was no hope; they both believed she had tried to terminate a pregnancy by taking a potion of some kind, and they had assured him the end was near. The Turkish healer said her womb was bleeding because it was rotten; the physician from Osijek said the bleeding had caused the rot.

Arandjel had been convinced from the start that a divorce was out of the question, that no priest or patriarch would take her from his brother and hand her over to him. Yet day after day he had promised his sister-in-law to go and see the Patriarch.

When she was taken ill, he began to act like a madman. All summer he was nowhere to be seen in the upper reaches of the Danube, not in Vienna or Buda, where he maintained large stocks of tanned leather and harnesses. At first he continued to take his barges and livestock as far as Osijek and Kovin, but he was always in a hurry, sailing at night and never pausing to say a word. After a fortnight or so he stopped going to Osijek, and even to Petrovaradin, stopped crossing the river into Turkey. Livid with rage at the losses he was incurring, he would pace the rooms of his large house on the water, gazing upon his sister-in-law as she slept and kissing her the moment she felt slightly better. Disgusted as he was by what was taking place, he nevertheless saw traces in her of the extraordinary beauty she had lost so abruptly. He withdrew his assets from Turkey and Walachia, abandoned his livestock trade, which would have meant leaving her alone, and concentrated entirely on silver. To silver he applied the same intrepid practices, the same principles of risk and plunder as he had to livestock and grain, yet he could spend most of his time at her side. Although he never reproached her outright for the losses she caused him, he made his feelings clear enough, always concluding with the great love he bore her, as if she owed him gratitude for it.

Sitting on her bed in his blue caftan and bright silk sash, he embraced her now-unattractive shoulders with his thin arms and tried to wheedle his yellowish eyes and pug nose into her good graces by tickling her with his beard and nudging her breasts with his head like a tame goat. But since she held him responsible for her illness and reacted coolly, he would remind her of that wanton night when he took her by force. His lips scented with a combination of expensive tobacco and Turkish delight, he went through their lovemaking, repeating his praise of the beauty of her limbs, the skill with which she moved, the fire with which she gave herself. He described it all to the last detail, his eyes burning, his voice rasping, then covered her with kisses.

Dame Dafina, who had never heard such things from her husband – for Vuk Isakovič was silent both during and after their lovemaking – paid little heed to her brother-in-law's babble and sweet talk; she found it burdensome. She would turn away, convulsed with pain, though receiving his fiery kisses with a smile – like the one she had smiled on that night – so vague that it did not reveal whether she felt any pleasure.

While her illness was in its early stages, it so repulsed him that he would flee. As time went on, however, he became quite attentive to her – partly out of fear, partly out of calculation. When her condition improved, he spent long hours plying her with kisses. When it deteriorated for good, he did not flee again; indeed, he spent the whole day by her bedside, rocking her in his arms for hours, as if in a trance.

She had lost her strength, yet he could not forget her legs; she had lost her passion, yet he still found her voice caressing, still thrilled with desire at her embrace. He never thought of taking another woman. Each time he told her the story of their first night together he told her what made her unique, different from all other women. Like a man bewitched, he lingered on the charms she had lost, and she wept.

In the end her illness not only ceased to repel him, it attracted him. His initial reserve turned into a kind of anticipation, strange and wonderful for him. Having taken so many women through hell, with Dafina he longed for heaven. Gazing into her eyes, he felt he could accept anything, even her death, the more so as a lifelong liaison with her had always seemed to him the height of folly.

Though accustomed to debauchery during his itinerant life in trade, Arandjel came to love his sister-in-law prior to her death with a pure, wholehearted love, the kind of love he had resisted for so long.

Shouting to his grooms from the window of the coach as it bumped and bounced at top speed along the back roads to Fruška Gora, he felt like a scarecrow sailing over the trees, bushes, and newly mown fields. He was preparing to fight and bargain with the priests, wheedle what he could from them.

Why he was going to expose his life to strangers, and how he hoped for the priests to help him when he had always maintained that confession was a worthless, ludicrous institution, he did not know. All he knew was that he had to do everything she asked, give her everything she requested. Even if he were eventually to flee from her, he would negotiate her divorce and accept her and his brother's children; even though he suspected she was after his money, he would present her with barges, livestock, houses – anything to show her he loved her before she died. Besides, at the mere thought that he might refuse her something, she rose up before him like a witch and made his life miserable with reprimands and abuse.

That he should handle his other affairs so well yet fail at this one irritated him greatly. All spring he had enjoyed extraordinary luck with his livestock – having fleeced half of Walachia – and after his brother's departure he had been looking forward to fantastic happiness with his sister-in-law: voluptuous pleasures and a secret life in his house on the water. She would be richly rewarded: he would keep her until his brother returned, or, if his brother failed to return, even longer. What he wanted most, after all the women he had had, was pleasure without female whims, without gifts of jewellery, dresses, ducats, without endless whining and pleading, tears and moans, without the torture. He had wanted to bask in a vast expanse of blue-green water that would filter the light of day and cradle his body, rock him like one of his boats when the wind was low, calmly, gently. Instead, here he was drowning again – he could not erase that incident from his memory – drowning with his horses, gulping sand and flailing in the mire. He had desired his sister-in-law for her exquisite beauty and vigour and did not anticipate any consequence of the sin, which he thought would remain hidden from the world. Far from the heavenly pleasures of a pasha's garden of delights, however, he experienced suffering more acute than he had ever imagined, and he was shaken, angered, crushed – and, in the end, profoundly saddened.

Hovering between rage and despair, he stubbornly refused to give up hope, even when he could see that it was all over. He did not fear his brother's return or feel remorse on his account; indeed, he never gave him a thought. Nor did he see that his sister-in-law had lost her happiness and her beauty at the very moment he took possession of her. He refused to accept the idea that so magnificent a woman could lose her beauty – those breasts, those shoulders, those legs and thighs – at least not until he had had his fill of them. When she howled in pain, he sent for the doctors and fled, but the moment her condition improved, he sat by her side for days, admiring her luminous forehead, her painfully smiling lips, her white ankles beautiful once again. She had to find salvation somewhere, he thought, she and he both, because he refused to accept the idea that the wonderful, carefree time he had planned to spend with her could end in the same cares and woes he had known with other women – or, worse, in agony and fear. He had believed that this time he would experience something other women were unable to give him, that for a while at least he would lead a good and beautiful life, much as his brother Vuk believed there was a good and beautiful land to which they should all migrate.

When he saw she was really dying. Arandjel Isakovič was so bewildered that his thoughts and desires fell into greater disarray than hers as she raved, or than his brother's as he wandered through the battlefield. Suppressing his impatience, he decided that all his misery would cease with her death: his sin would remain a secret, no one else would possess her, and the only true love in his life would reach a kind of luminous apotheosis which would keep it from sinking into anguish and pain. Besides, there were times when death seemed a necessary end to the turbulent thrashings of her extraordinary, voluptuous naked body. On the other hand, he had nothing to fear from her alive, and the thought of her dying after he had waited so long to possess her was so hateful, he felt he would surely perish as well, hurl himself into the water headfirst in despair, in disgrace, unable to live without her in that house, with those children, awaiting his brother. If he was to remain among the living once she had died, he would have to move far away, keep entirely to himself, fall silent, turn to stone.

The sole reason he was going to Karlovci was to make peace – that is, do her will – by bringing back a priest. Racing past meadows, swamps, and woodlands, he knew the journey was in vain, yet he pushed on at top speed. The poplars and acacias, their roots pounded by the wheels, took revenge by pummelling his head or scraping the windows with their branches.

Much less sensitive to the terrain than his brother, he went from shade into sunny plain without giving a thought to his dogs, who ran, panting, behind the coach, flushing larks from the surrounding underbrush. He sat straight and tall and paid no heed to the meadows or new settlements, pushing on, thinking only of himself and the house in which his sister-in-law lay dying. Not until the coach began the ascent to the Karlovci tollgate did he – exhausted, his face burned by the sun – fall back into the seat, close his eyes, and enjoy the ride through shady oak groves and past fragrant vineyards, bubbling brooks, and plum orchards whose branches dropped fruit in his wake.

Bumping in and out of ruts from rains long past, and tilting so precipitously that they were in constant danger of overturning, they came to the first houses, where the coach caused a great commotion among the populace, especially the dugout dwellers who had migrated from Serbia only seven years earlier to be with their Patriarch. Arandjel's father, Lazar Isakovič, was still fresh in their memories: they had tended his flocks and sold cattle for him as camp followers during the Austrian-Turkish campaign.

With its bells and fresh paint the coach had attracted

onlookers as it rushed up and down the nearby hills. Everyone ran to see it, as if it were a ship coming in. Arandjel's men riding ahead and those sitting on the coach box tried to appear straight-backed and inured to bumps, and the coachman cracked his whip imperiously and yelled at the crowds. He let up only when his master tossed handfuls of coins into the grass or thorns, though every time he did so, his dogs went wild and attacked people.

Reclining on his cushions, deep in thought, Arandjel never so much as glanced at them – more concerned with the live-stock, the sties, the roofs of the dugouts almost level with the ground. He was buying and selling it all, mentally. When the coach flew over ditches, he saw the rumps of his horses, their veins swollen by the effort, and when it got stuck, he saw his men leaping down, now to the left, now to the right, and chocking the wheels with blocks of wood.

By the time they reached the centre of town, a veritable procession of curiosity seekers, who would not be deterred, was trailing the coach. Stopping by a well under some plum trees, Arandjel continued on foot. He was used to being sur-rounded by people begging for alms, and allowed a certain number to approach and kiss his hand; he was even tolerant of those who ran up and, with tears in their eyes, grabbed his sleeve. They tagged along past vineyards and thickets, all the way to the house in which the Patriarch had taken up resi-dence for the summer.

Standing at the high gate inscribed with two crosses, telling his beads, bedecked in his rich raiments and scented, sur-rounded by his dogs and a swarm of the local poor, Arandjel Isakovič was aware he did not look the typical pilgrim. After surveying the neighbouring houses and roofs, he was granted entrance, but with only one servant. He bent his head as he stepped from the glaring light of day into the cool darkness of a large vaulted hall hung with icons, and told the monks who he was. He proceeded cautiously along the planks laid carefully on the earthen floor to a bench built into the wall, where the monks asked him to sit. But instead of taking him to the Patriarch, they stood and stared at him, perplexed.

The house was an old structure. It had a courtyard and stables and a plot of luxuriant grass with several apple trees, their branches so laden with fruit that they nearly touched the ground. Beyond the trees was a belfry made of logs, with a family of crows settled at the top and a long cord dangling from its clapper like a thick white snake. The courtyard was silent, the blue sky above it pure and constant.

Arandjel let his head drop: he was tired from the long journey and burdened by the thought that Dafina's life or peaceful death depended on his meeting with the Patriarch. The monks, moving like shadows along the wooden gallery or coming up to him in stolid silence, made him feel that no words needed to be said, that everything would happen of itself.

When he was finally told that he could not see the Patriarch because the Patriarch's sister, the wife of Colonel Rašković, and her daughters had just arrived for a visit, he arose from the bench, offended. Though only of medium height and quite slender, he appeared much more substantial and imposing. One of the monks lowered his eyes and added that the Patriarch had been having trouble with his eyes and was lying prostrate in the darkness of his cell, his eyelids covered, praying to God and seeing no one.

Arandjel Isakovič opened his jacket and threw out a chest arrayed in multicoloured silks and costly jewels. In an exaggeratedly gentle and unassuming voice he repeated his name, mentioned his brother, Vuk Isakovič, and stated his business, namely, that he wished to speak personally to the Patriarch, with whom he had had the honour to converse at length twice, the previous winter.

Hearing the name Vuk Isakovič, the monks became suddenly animated. They praised and blessed his valour, his

155

generosity to them, his determination to uphold the Orthodox faith. Their tributes made of him a saint on horseback, defending poor innocent monks and the fugitives from blood-soaked Serbia, and ready to do even more once he returned from the wars.

After sending the monks back to the Patriarch, he wondered, Do they know I am a fornicator? Have they heard anything? Staring out at the apple trees and the wooden belfry, he regretted having come. He saw that they could not help him, that they knew all about the life he led on his boats and abroad, that no matter how generous he was to the church, they despised him. He thought he saw the face of the Patriarch – its long, ear-to-ear beard, clipped moustache, and crafty eyes – in a second-floor window, and he was certain he was being watched from other windows. He was so incensed and ashamed that he crossed his legs Turkish-style and began to smoke.

The monks returned with the message that the Patriarch was unable to grant Arandjel Isakovič an audience but would send one of his monks to his ailing wife, and that he advised him to talk with Bishop Nenadovič, whom he knew well, about the matter of importance Isakovič had wished to discuss with him.

Arandjel lost his temper. With a bitter, sardonic smile he accused them of acting worse than soldiers, who spill innocent blood and live like Gypsies, and of forcing people to migrate and preventing honest merchants and artisans from living in peace and quiet. He called his brother, whom they had lauded so, the worst kind of Gypsy, who hid his indolence behind a never-ending stream of promises of a new and better life in Russia. Then he lit into the Patriarch, shocking the monks by calling him – the former Archbishop of Pécs and current Patriarch of all the Serbs in Hungary, Serbia, Bulgaria, Bosnia, Greece, Dalmatia, Croatia, Slavonia, and Illyria – an old skin-flint, who would yet have need of his, Arandjel Isakovič's, fortune, which fortune he then demonstrated by pouring two pouches of ducats into his lap and counting out how much he had planned to donate for the construction of the Patriarch's new church, how much for the bells, how much for the portrait of Tsar Uroš the Meek of blessed memory, how much for the upkeep of the monastery, and, finally, how much for the monks themselves. He sighed deeply as he spoke, and the monks sniffed their basil with increasing frequency.

He mentioned in passing that though a mere merchant, he was in no way less worthy than his brother, Vuk, because despite his brother's reputation as a soldier, all he did was talk and make promises, while he, Arandjel, worked hard, bought and sold, and had something to show for it. One day they would see through his brother, Vuk, who would send them back to the plains and hills and swamps and woods to die like dogs on their way to Russia, the land they knew nothing about. Then they would understand why he, Arandjel, wanted no more than to stay where he was, on the land where they had settled, stay on the land and buy it up, and, just as he gave money to the men who worked for him, he would give money to the church and much more than his brother would. Standing at the door now, he felt deeply humiliated, as if someone had emptied a bucket of cold water on his head. He then played the merchant's trick of adjusting his wide sleeves, making ready to rise. The monks, however, failed to respond; they were utterly confused, understanding neither what so enraged him nor what he was trying to say. He pushed on: he knew that people were talking about his sister-in-law's living in his house in Zemun, but the fact was that with his brother away at war, someone had to take care of his poor sickly daughters; besides, his sister-in-law was on her deathbed, which was why he needed to talk to the Patriarch.

One of the monks offered to deliver his request yet again, but Isakovič had reached the point of singing his own praises and would brook no interruption. He was the merchant in the family, he said in his squeaky voice, the one who knew how to make money and keep it. Whose money did they think his brother gave to the church? And who did they think would keep what they made, if not he and the people he had settled up and down the river, settled there for good? For property belongs to people who live in one place, not to people who move around like Gypsies. People who can withstand a livestock pestilence without weeping and moaning can withstand anything. They will not leave. Had anyone seen Arandjel Isakovič bat an eye when his barges went down or his herds were plundered? True, he had a reputation as a libertine, a man who bought his women, but since when did that keep a man from becoming a benefactor of the church? Could he not reform and live the life of a saint? As soon as he returned to Zemun, he would send them a cartful of icons far more beautiful than the ones in their vault, and as for their belfry – to which he gave a contemptuous glance – the one he had built for his village was higher and had a stone base. They could go and tell that to their Patriarch.

As his eyes moved from the wooden belfry and its mute bell to the still trees with their countless apples and on to the stables and second-floor windows where there was no movement, he began to feel he had spoken too long and too loud for the cool dark vault with its icons and icon lamps. He resolutely walked out of the gate and emerged before the crowd, shouting at his servant and surrounded by monks, who did everything they could to prevent his departure.

The crowd now included a number of ragged, almost naked Gypsies hopping up and down and begging piteously for alms. Arandjel's servants and their whips notwithstanding, they followed him back to his coach. The coach set off immediately, climbing past gullies and fields as if soaring over the rooftops, over thatched eaves and pigsties and stakes pounded into the ground, over enormous tree trunks and their rambling roots.

From above, the town appeared nestled in a reedy marshland. Farther off stretched a patch of felled woods, the wide river lined by willows on both banks, and, beyond the willows, an endless plain. The sun beat down so mercilessly that the coach seemed plated with red-hot iron as it made its way, accompanied by the panting dogs, over the bumpy road to the orchards of Bishop Nenadovič. The Bishop had erected a small wooden chapel next to his house and gathered together a small group of hermit monks who had agreed to give up their solitary lives in the surrounding woods and vineyards and join the brotherhood in the heart of Fruška Gora.

On the way to the Bishop's orchards, Arandjel decided not to bring up the divorce or his unsuccessful attempt to see the Patriarch, but simply to request that the Bishop do everything in his power to relieve the torment of his sister-in-law's final hours, which torment he had allowed to slip his mind momentarily. He would ask for a monk to go with him to Zemun, and tell the monk to introduce himself to Dafina as a special envoy from the Patriarch. Otherwise there would be more of the feverish screams and mad whispers with which she had sent him off.

It occurred to him that he had done no trading for weeks. His life would never be the same now; he would never be cheerful or happy again. When she died, there would be nothing left for him. Reclining on the cushioned seat, he thought back enviously to the days when he had little to do with her, and to his once firm resolution to enjoy her no more than two or three times.

Meanwhile the coach, which had been rolling along a dried-up ditch, came to a bridge made of logs and branches. Feeling the bridge sway and shake underfoot, the horses reared. It was all the men could do to keep them from overturning the coach.

Arandjel rose and saw a stand of old acacias interspersed with bushes so thick – a profusion of weeds at their base, nourished by spring freshets but now dry, gave off a heavy odour of putrefaction – that they blocked the path. Beyond them, at the far end of a gently sloping meadow speckled with fruit-laden pear trees, stood the Bishop's large yellow house, the roof of the nearby wooden chapel emerging from the crowns of stately oaks, which were far enough apart to afford a view of the meadows, vineyards, and distant woods in the valley below. Uncertain how best to approach the house, he was about to order his men to axe their way through the thicket when his eye fell on a strange black silhouette against a tree.

It was a young monk, sitting motionless at the foot of an acacia, his tattered robe open, his body bent forward in fervent prayer. Suddenly he crossed himself several times, raised his arms to the sky, and, writhing in silence like a demon, thrust his chest, his stomach, his back at the point of a sharp stake of acacia wood set in the ground in front of him. It was some time before Arandjel noticed that he was crying.

While the coachmen did their best to calm the horses and push the wheels back to firm ground, Arandjel shuddered at the thought of the monk's pain, though the man appeared to feel it not at all. Watching the awful contortions, he heard a scream – a scream that made the horses rear again and the monk start as from the lash of a whip – and was surprised to recognize it as his own.

The tall, barefoot monk came up to him, his face haggard, his large eyes cloudy and feverish, blood dripping down his chest, and indicated with an angry gesture that the coach would have to go around the trees to reach the road leading to the Bishop's house. Once his men managed to move the coach back, the horses, though still trembling, found the stone gate in no time. But Arandjel could not take his eyes off the madman, who, obsessed with the idea of impaling himself, was once more flailing in pain, writhing over his stake as if embracing it, with no thought whatever of the hot summer day beyond the acacias, the grassy meadows, swamps, homesteads, and stone structures bedecked with iron roosters below him.

As the coach passed through the gate and pulled up to the large house, an elderly prior came out to meet it. He immediately assured Arandjel that the Bishop was at home, in the garden. The man praying at the stake, he said, was a monk by the name of Pantelejmon, who had recently come from Serbia. Seven years ago today his entire family had been impaled before his eyes as they fled the Turks. He was now insane. The reason he made no sound was that the Turks had pulled out his tongue. There was no need to fear him: he was meek and mild; he just cried all the time.

On his way into the house Arandjel paused on the raised wooden veranda to gaze at the river and the sun burning down on the distant reeds and marshes with such intensity that thick black smoke rose from them. Left alone in a room where there was nothing but a mural of John the Anchorite carrying an axe, he walked over to the window. He saw three monks. One of them, enormously fat, was sprawled on his stomach asleep, his head buried in the grass; the other two – one auburn-haired and as soft and fair as a girl, the second swarthy and bearded – were sitting back to back, humming and playfully grabbing at each other's throats over their shoulders. On that side of the house, the woods were only steps away.

Tired and hungry, drenched with sweat, Arandjel could feel the chill penetrate his bones as he leaned against the cold wall. He heard steps approaching. Fingering his beads and muttering almost deliriously, he decided to tell the Bishop that he had brought him ten ducats for the monasteries and ten for vestments and to ask him to gain his sister-in-law admission to the convent at Jazak, where the waters might do her good. He would also tell him that he had taken her from his brother, that he had made her pregnant, and that he did not wish to part from her.

What he actually told the Bishop, whom he had known since the latter's days as a clerk at the Buda Court, and what he did during the rest of his stay at the Bishop's summer residence, where strict community rule prevailed over the vagaries of hermit life, Arandjel Isakovič never told a soul, not even in his difficult old age, when he was known far and wide as a vile miser. But when his grooms drove him home that evening, dead drunk – he had never been so drunk – they heard him mumble that he would be leaving all his money to the church, which was what they too should do when the time came, for life in heaven was the only life worth living, and that the next day he would be taking Dame Dafina to Jazak, where the waters would certainly cure her. While the coach was passing through the Karlovci tollgate and the soldiers came running because they mistook him for a general from Petrovaradin, he added that when he grew old, or perhaps earlier, he would have himself tonsured and become a hermit, resting from his labours in a modest hut, free from all those damned Walachians and clubfooted Greeks. Lolling on his back and singing the livelong day, he would at last be at peace. If he felt like wine, he would have it, and if a nice plump peasant girl happened past, he would trip her with his staff, she would lose her balance, and into his hut she would fly. Much as he praised the Bishop, he rejected the community life, wishing to be alone with his God. Yet he praised the monks, spoke of them as though he had spent his life among them, and assured his men that he was on better terms with the monks who guarded Prince Brankovič's relics than his brother Vuk was, and that they had explained to him wherein he had sinned and then pardoned him.

Since he had never spoken at length to his men before, they not only failed to pay attention but even tried not to listen. They feared that once he was sober he would sorely repent of having let slip more than necessary and consequently would torture them for weeks.

And, indeed, the moment the evening breezes reached him, he fell silent. Silent, he watched as the coach descended to the marshland, to the Danube, leaving the houses of

Karlovci behind on the hill, still gleaming in the sun. In the cool semidarkness of the woods, reeds, and grasses, he listened to his dogs barking at skylarks and chasing quail.

At one point the men made a stop to ready their rifles and pistols, the road ahead being less than safe. Arandjel began to feel the effects of his intoxication again and moved around restlessly, even tried to climb the wrought-iron ornamentation on the coach. He must have heard something heartening at the Bishop's, because he not only started praising him again but also kept trying to sing a song he had learned there. His voice had a screechy quality and seemed louder than normal; the men cringed at the sound of it. Then he shed tears over Pantelejmon's impaled family, vowed once more to become a monk, and ran through the saints in whose names he had given the Bishop ducats. He reiterated his confidence in the curative powers of the convent waters, and even predicted that Dafina would be able to bear children again. Many children. He would make peace with his brother. They *were* brothers, after all, even if Vuk always got the better of him.

The thought that Dafina might be saved – could the doctors have only imagined that her illness was fatal? – filled him with such joy that he nearly started to dance in the coach. Stretching out his arms to the increasingly brisk evening, he racked his brain to bring back everything he had said to the monks and everything they had said to him, but his mind was on Dafina.

No dealings in Arandjel Isakovič's life had ever gone so wrong as his dealings with her. The outcome had caught him completely off guard. In a different, more acute way than his brother he sensed the horror, the true horror of their migratory existence, the absurd instability that ensured that nothing happened according to their will or expectations. More and more he wished that he and his brother might be reconciled and flee to that new land, swampy and flat, yet fragrant and heavenly, to settle at last after all their wanderings. When earlier on he was wild with desire for her, he never dreamed his desire would one day be consummated. And now he was watching her die in his house. He found it unspeakable that at first he intended to have his way with her in secret and send her back to his brother. The mere thought of her magnificent body, her cool limbs and undulating hips, made the idea of giving her up to his brother ridiculous. He would no more have let anyone take his place next to her than he would have let anyone take his place were he able to walk across the glittering blue river or above the trees or through the sky.

It was as though all the other women, the myriad women with whom, panting, sweating, drunk as often as not, he had coupled – fair women, swarthy women, women with red hair and ample bosoms who breathed deeply and sniffled softly in his embrace – had remained behind on the other side of the river, while she was here with him, in the coach, by his side, unique, with her wonderful fragrance, her smooth skin, her eyes the colour of a clear winter sky.

If she now gave birth instead of dying, which Arandjel in his drunken stupor thought perfectly possible, all their troubles would be over, and he would be a hero not only to himself but also to her, his brother, everyone. All he needed was to see her healthy, feel the frenzy of being near her, opening her thighs, dancing attendance on her. Even if she were as cold as stone, as cold as on that first night, in his intoxication he perceived her as a magnificent apparition, and sank into mindlessness, certain that the coach taking him through the moonlit fields was taking him straight to paradise.

But the journey home would last the entire night; he had hours to go. On his left he felt the chill of the swamp and heard the swish of the reeds, which had dried up during the long drought and looked like phantoms in the moonlight. The willow-lined river beyond seemed to be standing still. Whenever they came to a thicket, they were met by swarms of fireflies. The ground was so hard from want of rain that the horseshoes rang hollow and the horses seemed to be crossing one long bridge. He could watch the regular motion of their legs until morning in the eerie light of a lantern hanging from one of the shafts, the motion of their legs and those of the exhausted dogs.

On his right he saw field after field of tall grass, dotted now and then with villages, he guessed from the barking heard as they passed, and then total darkness, the kind of darkness that bodes certain death. Above the water, where there was much light upon the surface of the earth, the sky was dark, fathomless, invisible; above the black plains, above the dense grasses, the sky was high, dark blue, and sparkled with stars.

Listening to the coach bells, gazing up at the night sky and out into the grass as far as the lantern cast its light, and following the ghostlike shadows that, faceless in the dark, may or may not have been his men, Arandjel Isakovič, increasingly sober, became a new man.

The plan of asking the Patriarch to hear his confession, which was dictated partly by his father's friendship with Metropolitan Jovanovič, now seemed utter folly, and the confession he had made to Bishop Nenadovič and the comfort the Bishop had given him by drinking with him and taking his pouch of ducats for the maintenance of the monastery belonged to another world. The church and its wooden belfries and icons calling to him in a supernal whisper gave him no more relief than any of the worldly things he had encountered that day. Riding through the night in his coach, he left all vain hope behind and, convinced he would have done better to have said nothing, came back to himself. Like his brother on the battlefield, so he with this woman suddenly felt his former life fall away from him, leaving him alone, completely alone, with whatever lay ahead until death.

The stocks of hides and tobacco, the silver, the debtors — everything he had delighted in contemplating seemed lost forever in that night. The houses, the sties, the costly raiment were as nothing compared with the blade of grass that grazed his hand as it hung out of the coach. The bargains he had struck, the money he had lent far and wide, and his self-esteem had neither meaning nor value among the dry moonlit swamps.

Terrified by the prospect that he would find her dead and live out his life in mourning, he began to wonder, like his brother, whether everything was not in fact a dream. Although he had never thrown away a piece of gold or silver – except the small coins he scattered among the poor when in a holiday mood – he now thought how pleasant it would be to throw away the ducats he carried in his belt. Trembling with anguish and pleasure, he let them filter through his fist and drop noiselessly into the grass.

Only now did he see that his attempts to make her part of society, to make her more than his shadow in that awful room of hers, were doomed from the start. The Bishop had winced at the mere mention of her name. Arandjel would have done better to say nothing.

Clearly, the life he had made the bedrock of his existence – a life of accounts, machinations, and profits, of travelling, plundering, and whoring – was over. He had always assumed he could arrange everything and take his pleasures accordingly, and if that meant constantly cheating and hurting people, it only led him to despise people from the depths of his soul. Yet he was now as much a fool as they, and as much despised.

Now he realized there was another life, a life invisible to the eye and unfathomable to the mind, a life whose most trivial detail he could not arrange, yet which was as bright and shining as the light on the road, the threads of moonlight reaching from heaven to earth and back again. Even though everything that happened in that life happened by mere mad chance, it glittered with events of astral significance for both body and soul. No one could disturb him in that life, secret and unpredictable, and there he and his sister-in-law could yield completely to their stunning sensuality, secure in the thought that no one was watching.

In the course of his journey home that night, at the end of the summer during which he had satisfied the most ardent desire in his life, Arandjel Isakovič, much like his brother, Vuk, on the battlefield of a far-off land, aged more in several hours than he had in several years.

By dawn, when they came to Zemun, he was lying in the coach, pale and weak, his chin trembling like an old goat's, his eyes no longer on the stars, which had faded, nor did he notice the daylight glimmering in the heights. But when he saw the belfries of the town loom in the distance, he called out one last time to his men, who had fallen asleep in a sitting position, and to the horses, which were now good for nothing. He stood and looked out over the roofs and water mills along the river with utter indifference. He felt he was about to awake from the dream that had been his life and start a new, completely different one.

As they crossed the bridge in front of his house, with a sad, gentle smile, he greeted the crowd that had gathered there, and concluded from their tearful eyes that she was dying. No sooner did his sallow hand and the sleeve of his coat touch the gate than all the servants burst into great sobs and lamentations, beating their chests. The house reeked of candles.

Dame Dafina, clean, calm, her eyes open, her arms crossed over her breasts, lay covered with silks like a white ghost, her stern, terrifying glance fixed on the door. Arandjel dismissed the women; he did not want her to see them. He did not realize that she could see no longer, that she had not recognized him, that at the very moment he took her in his arms she would expire.

He pressed her and her pillow to his chest, rocking her and weeping. He flailed out at anyone who came near, even the servants trying to close her eyelids, which were now tinged with blue. The candle they had placed in her hands fell over and burned him. He was like a madman, and his shadow on the wall like the monk writhing over the stake, the black monk he had watched the day before, incredulous.

Not until he looked deeply into Dafina's eyes, those two motionless winter-sky-blue orbs that grew as he approached them, not until then did he regain his equilibrium. Her eyes were all that was left him, and he would never forget their colour. In his sister-in-law's last breath he saw the sky. And like his brother in his dream, he too, in terror and grief, saw blue circles, and in them a star.

He fell into delirium over her dead body, madly mumbling prayers and wailing: "Dafina my love, my love, it's your Arandjel, your Arandjel," like a sheep bleating. No matter how the women screamed, they could not tear him away from their dead mistress.

As for Dafina, who could neither see nor hear all this but lay inert, with a string of the fine pearls of death-agony sweat adorning her forehead – Dame Dafina, otherworldly and radiant in a flurry of snowflakes and flames, in a mingling of Slavonian woods and heavenly constellations, saw the face of Vuk Isakovič.

9

*One of Them, the Most Wretched of All, Retained the
Radiance of His Being Even After Death, and Was Able
to Return and Appear at the Entrance to the Village,
at the Place by the Road Where the First Acacias
Bloom Every Spring*

For months the Slavonian villages received no word from their
men who had gone to war. They had vanished, disappeared
into the clouds.

In earlier times, when the Turks were the enemy, the
people would see villages being razed to the ground and
Turkish boats packed with slaves plying the rivers; they would
hear of monasteries in flames, women raped, children flung
into the air and caught on daggers. Not a word of that now.
The men who had gone were doubtless fighting somewhere,
though God knew where: in lands whose names they did not
know and with armies they could not picture. The stories told
around the fire were ghastly, bloodcurdling, much worse than
the ones about the massacres and atrocities of the Turks. All
they could see when they turned in the direction Vuk Isakovič
and his men had taken were the great abyss of a river lined
with willows and, now, the dark-grey, rainy sky.

The early reports – that some of the men had been sent to
France, while others, the men from Varadin, were in Prussia
– stunned them. They wailed with fear and sorrow at the
thought that their men had been separated, divided, and
would not even be allowed to die together. It was all so

confusing and strange: the men were fighting with all kinds of people, passing through all kinds of countries, each with its own climate and rivers and woods and the queerest of customs. And they would be away for years. Rumour also had it that many of the men had taken new brides, that they would not be returning, that they had even had children. By early autumn their wives were not only weeping and wailing but cursing too.

The first real news was that Sekula – whom they all knew, because he was one of Isakovič's orderlies and the bell ringer and sexton of a village church – had been flogged to within an inch of his life. People were shocked. There was talk that he would be sent home, that he had lost an eye and had both ears burned off, or that his face was all bone, like the head of a skinned ram.

Then came the widely spread report that the body of Prince Djuradj Brankovič had been brought back from abroad and buried at Fruška Gora. Even the most isolated villages trembled with anxiety, as if suspended in the turbulent but luminous air of a rare sunny late-autumn day.

There were other dire reports from time to time, but not always reliable, especially with regard to names and the train of events: that Vuk Isakovič's regiment had been exterminated, for example. The reports circulating in the villages where Vuič had recruited his two regiments were even darker. And when people learned what had happened to the men who were fighting in Bohemia under Colonel Raškovič, the keening and lamentations reached far across the plains beyond the Danube.

To make matters worse, the land on which they had settled and lived in peace, and which had been fertile and fruitful all summer because the swamps were dry, had with autumn's fitful rains and floods brought back anguished, desperate thoughts of migration. Their livestock drowned, their wells went bad, their sties washed away, their villages were covered with toppled trees and newly mown grass, their fences were broken, their paths turned into beds of muck and mire, and everywhere there was mud – mud weighing down roofs, mud seeping into huts and dugouts. The woods they had cleared, the swamps they had cultivated all the way to the warm and fertile slopes had returned to the state they found them in when they arrived.

Willows rose in the mist; clouds tumbled lower and lower. The river ran through dark and impenetrable depths. The earth was black, invisible, swollen with rain. The marshes hummed and buzzed in the night, sending the light of the moon back through the willows, where it disappeared into the gloom.

The place where Vuk Isakovič's father had settled and built houses on the slope of a hill, and whence Vuk had set off with his boats, suffered from the flooding more than most. Every day the rains lashed at the hill, carrying off topsoil, palings, and ricks of dried grass to the swampland below. A wide crack developed in the northern wall of the Isakovič house, and unless the rains let up, the entire structure would collapse. The meadow surrounding it, high above the Danube, was saturated, and so riddled with holes and crevices that the livestock kept tripping and falling. Dense clumps of tall, slender reeds swayed at the foot of the hill. In the wooded area beyond the meadow, partially cleared by Vuk's soldiers, were the dugouts of families waiting to build mud huts along the river in the village, whose church had a wooden belfry with icons brought from the old homesteads of the Vukovič and Isakovič families under its roof.

Vuk's village was usually the first to receive news from abroad. People there were the first to hear that his orderly Arkadije had died and that the body had never been recovered. They also heard that many others had died, including several officers, and that Maria Theresa had sent the soldiers a thaler each for their bravery. For a time there was talk of the death of the rich Antonovič, for whom the merchants of Temesvár later built a church on the hill above his village, overlooking the Petrovaradin entrenchments. And when the villagers heard that men had been hanged for stealing apples, cries and lamentations again spread over the land.

But as the summer came to an end, the common topic of conversation was the death of Dame Dafina, and her life.

Everyone knew what had caused her death, and everyone looked upon it as retribution for Arandjel Isakovič's sins and wanton deeds. People said that all of moneyed Zemun had rushed to see her on her deathbed, both because of her beauty and because of the precious silks and jewels she wore even in death. The villagers wept at the thought that the funeral would be too far away for them to attend it; they heard that people were planning to cross the river from Turkey to partake of the funeral banquet in Arandjel Isakovič's house. But then came the great quarrel.

The Greek clergy of Zemun asserted that the Christodoulos family had always been faithful and widely recognized bene-factors of the Greek church and that Dafina should therefore be buried by Greek priests in the Greek cemetery, under the church threshold; Arandjel Isakovič, on the other hand, said that although her mother's second husband – she had married him while abroad – was a Greek, her true father was a pure-blooded Serb, and she should therefore be buried according to the new rites of the Serb clergy.

When the villagers, all of whom knew Vuk Isakovič, learned that the mean and spiteful Arandjel had refused to hand his sister-in-law's body over to the Greek priests and was planning to bury her on the hill behind Vuk's house, next to Lazar Isakovič's grave, where it would be visible far and wide, even from the plain, their joy was boundless. And so all the people who had wept and wailed as they saw Vuk Isakovič go off to war were now able to weep and wail to their hearts' content as they saw his wife go to her grave. And brief as the funeral

172

service was, the crowd, weary from want and war rumours, was satisfied. They had seen Arandjel's coach and his horses; they had seen his outlandishly dressed servants; they had even caught a glimpse of the yellow-eyed, pug-nosed Arandjel, looking like a pasha in his silk sashes, white stockings, gold buckles, and brocades, fingering his rosary in one bony golden-ringed hand and tossing silver coins to the poor along his way, more generous than ever before.

Thus did Dafina pass one last time by the hut where she had spent her last, turbulent, night with her husband. The coffin containing her body lay open on the veranda under a white-washed ceiling hung with garlands of onions and maize. Amid much keening and lamenting, the villagers who wished to see the coffin climbed up to the veranda in their bare feet on large sacks of dried beans, among them a number of old men so feeble that their first sip of *rakija* made them drunk, and old women who grabbed the corpse's arm and, screaming, kissed it.

While the priest performed the service, Arandjel Isakovič stood bareheaded behind the coffin, under a roof covered with pigeons, and all eyes were on him. His face was wrinkled; he looked ill, in need of sleep. He glanced around absently, deep in thought. He felt he was doing right by his brother to bury Dafina near the house where they had lived in wedlock rather than near his own. As long as the mourners came up to kiss her hand, he stood motionless over the body, seeing nothing, hearing nothing.

Certain that her death would not take him by surprise, here he was, amazed to find her dead. His head bent, his eyes were fixed on his hands, empty hands, as if a turtledove had just escaped from them. Then suddenly he shuddered and wept.

Suddenly, there in his brother's house, he felt that he and he alone was to blame for everything, he and his base desire for his sister-in-law's body, his deceitful plan of settling her in his house the better to gain access to her while his brother was away at war. Vuk had been fated to go to war, Dafina fated to fall ill and die only that he might have her briefly, and all this vain, entangled suffering had come to pass only that he might satisfy for an instant the hunger of his loins.

Still he could not accept the idea that she was dead, that it was over. He went on thinking about her, whispering about her, about her body, as if he were soon to see it, stroke it, possess it again. He kept staring at the coffin, at the candles illuminating it, at the woman stretched out in it, and thinking that she was the only woman who had ever remained desirable to him beyond the night when she satisfied his desire.

Her eyes – the large blue orbs illuminating everything around her even as she breathed her last – lived in his mind, retained their shimmer in his soul. With her he had found more than debauchery and pleasure; he had found something everlasting, something that lifted him above life and into the eternal blue. Instead of wasting his time in trade – weighing silver, selling cattle – he could have been touched by marvels, like the tip of a silver fir emerging from the soil, brushing against his chest in the total darkness in which he now expected to live.

At last the coffin was carried up the hill and lowered into the ground. The servants could barely guide Arandjel Isakovič to the coach: he was numb, unable to walk.

After Dafina's burial and Arandjel Isakovič's departure, the village at the foot of the hill sank back into autumn. Rain oozed through the walls, poured down from the roofs in torrents; vegetation rotted in the mud. Huts and dugouts were invaded by frogs; water seeped into bedding. For days on end there was no one to be seen on the hill or along the banks of the river; all there was, from earth to sky, over hills and willows and dreary lowlands, was misty rain.

Arandjel's old curmudgeon of a servant, Ananije, had with his wife and daughters moved large quantities of straw and hay, and whole ricks of maize up to Vuk's house. Wearing nothing but an overcoat and underwear and surrounded by dogs, he slept by the threshold as before, but with so many blankets it was impossible to tell his head from his feet until morning, when he began to wriggle like a pig in a sack, and out came two bright blue eyes, a tangle of beard and eyebrows. He spent whole days seeking dry spots from which to look out at the rainy horizon and watch the village, its mud huts and much neglected livestock and harvest, go to ruin. He settled on the open veranda, not wishing to force the door; he would move inside only if Vuk Isakovič failed to return.

Ananije's pale, sickly face bore the traces of all he had seen and did not dare tell. His wife and daughters knew nothing; he knew everything. He knew why Dafina had been brought to his master's house and what Arandjel had done with her; he had observed her illness and her death at close quarters; he had seen things neither Arandjel nor his sister-in-law dreamed he saw. He had served Arandjel Isakovič for many years and knew his master's concubines as he knew his business schemes. Nor did it escape his attention that for some time his own two elder daughters would suddenly dart out of Arandjel's bedroom, but he knew they were not comely enough for that to provide him with a prosperous old age. He had taken over his master's deadly greed for silver and wore a ribbon strung with silver pieces around his bare waist. Though there was a time when he would not have hurt a fly or slaughtered a sheep – saying it was a sin to shed blood – he had become the wiliest and most merciless predator, feared by all, from sties to barges, for the sordid intrigues he spun to blacken the reputation of anyone he chose with Arandjel. He had neither male progeny nor male family, yet he had acquired a great deal of arable land and was acquiring more.

Dafina's arrival had been a severe blow to him, her death a welcome event. His hopes were kindled anew. He had learned the art of waiting from his master, and he now waited for his

175

master to notice his youngest daughter, who had begun to come into her own. Her ample breasts and thighs were just what Arandjel valued most in a woman, but although she took to parading them before his faded goggle-eyes – bending before him, touching his hands – it was, to Ananije's great surprise, in vain.

With Dafina's arrival Arandjel had grown strange, and with her illness he grew even stranger. Women no longer existed for him, and his eyes, once as bright and yellow as a cat's, had clouded over and seemed always to be looking up and beyond Ananije's head. After Dafina's death, when Arandjel called for him, Ananije took his youngest daughter along, but again he saw his hopes dashed: gone were the moist red lips redolent of Turkish delight, the voluptuary's reserved smile, the fire in the glance as it measured each woman from head to toe. What he saw instead was a morose insomniac who went for days on end without saying a word. He watched Arandjel through the cracks in the door: hunched and staring at his empty hands for hours.

If he revealed his master's secrets to no one, he was all the more talkative about the curious events leading up to Dafina's death: how she screamed when she saw her husband walking on the water through the dark in the shape of a frog spouting blood, or lying on his bed split in two, or whole again but in her white stove, his eyes dangling from their sockets. He was a fine storyteller, one who knew how to give his listeners gooseflesh. He would tell how Arandjel, shortly after she arrived, had nearly drowned when his horses crushed him in the river and filled his mouth with their manes, and how a combination of cockroaches and ants had devoured a hand of the servant who did her hair, and how the house had been overrun with snakes, which seemed to prefer laying their young under her bed. Furthermore, Ananije was absolutely certain she would rise from her grave and haunt the village.

Throughout the rainy, muddy days, when mist hung over

the land like smoke and the reeds and willows sank ever deeper into water, and the pitch-black nights, when families slept huddled together under piles of pelts reeking of sheep and kept a lamp burning, Dame Dafina became the village ghost. Thanks to Ananije, she began to poison the water in the wells, inflict pestilences upon the livestock, and spread maladies of the chest and entrails that no one could explain. The sheep were struck first, then the hogs; then women's breasts began to ache. That Dafina had lain with her husband's brother became common knowledge, as did the odious secrets of her life in his house and the details of her illness – especially after a strangled infant of unknown parentage was found at the entrance to the village.

At last the rain let up and fine autumn weather set in over the barren yellow fields and stagnant ponds, and at night, when the moonlight shone through the woods and crept down the hill, Dafina galloped through the village on a hoe and flew up into the mulberry trees. Someone saw her crouching on the well sweep behind Vuk Isakovič's house. She was big and white.

Sheep disappeared in unprecedented numbers, and their owners would find them at Vuk Isakovič's house. Fights broke out as fear grew, and women took an active part. Every night Dafina perched on their fat peasant stomachs and squeezed their necks between her knees; in the morning they had dysentery, chills, and the pox. On the night of the first snow a pregnant woman saw Dafina standing by her stable in the shape of a white cow, and she fell dead.

Only Arandjel Isakovič – who visited the grave in his coach and ordered a wooden shelter erected and decorated with icons he had brought with him – retained his image of Dafina, of her smooth skin, sweet flesh, and luminous shoulders. For everyone else she was a large white apparition. A vampire. Before long nearly everyone in the village had encountered it, the culmination of the woes visited upon them since Vuk

Isakovič had taken the best men off to war. People stopped gathering at the belfry for prayers; daughters-in-law came under attack; fathers-in-law wrestled all night with the invisible enemy; old women, climbing the hill in the morning to the well, told one another all sorts of horror stories, crossing themselves faster and faster. Only a bolt of lightning could save the village, they agreed.

The wife of Vuk's orderly Arkadije came in for a particularly large share of the talk. Stana, for such was her name, moved with her infant into the hut near the sties, where Dafina had spent her last night with her husband. She mended the thatched roof so that it no longer leaked and stuffed branches into the holes in the door so that frogs no longer hopped over the earth floor; she spread out a bed by the stove, a bed that could accommodate a great deal.

After living alone for months, mourning her husband and rebuffing the overtures of Vuk's shepherds, who milked their sheep in front of her door, she gave in one hot night, languid from a large portion of warm milk one of them had poured for her. So taken was the poor man with her charms that he told all his comrades about her, and one by one they took his place in her bed.

Just as in a corner of the horizon, when all else is autumn gloom, there may be a beautiful patch of blue, so in the mire of Vuk Isakovič's village, amid the swamps and reeds, the stumps and pits and ditches, there was now a patch of paradise that men could enter as they pleased. The tall, thick grass surrounding it served as a natural screen. Pumpkins grew by the door; a young mulberry tree arched above the roof. The view from the threshold stretched over the river and beyond. The earth fairly radiated warmth. The baby's crying did not deter Stana's lovers; indeed, it seemed to attract them. They came in an unending procession.

Timid by nature, Stana was prone to shriek at the slightest provocation, and when one day at sunrise she saw the vampire on her threshold, Ananije, whose daughters were close friends of hers, had to promise her that he would plunge a hawthorn stake into Dafina's grave on the night of the next full moon.

Thus it was that to calm both dogs and villagers, Ananije sallied forth on the fateful night to plunge a hawthorn stake into Dafina's grave.

Standing bareheaded on the veranda before leaving, he sniffed the falling night as a dog sniffs an approaching stranger. Smoke rose along the horizon from purple plains and restless cattails under a broad, bright yellow sky, but the river flowed black within its banks, making him feel that he was in total darkness. Peering into the night, he observed the wind winding through the grasses, and the cold in the eyes of the dogs gathered around him. Slowly the bleating of the herds and the shouting of the herdsmen died away.

Only his wife and daughters knew his purpose – and Arkadije's wife, for Stana came to call daily, squatting with the other women by the fire late into the night, roasting peas and pumpkins with them and recounting her amorous adventures as if they had happened to other women from the village.

As soon as the moon came out, Ananije climbed the fence, armed with a mallet and the hawthorn stake. He nearly turned back when he saw how strange the fields, woods, and hills looked rising up before him. The women, who had been telling his fortune, waited until he climbed the fence, then followed. They cried out in fear when they saw him slow his step, and breathed easy only when he called back to them softly that there was no danger. They followed him up the hill, whispering worriedly, constantly crossing themselves, always in the full moonlight, while he strode forth bravely, yet in the shadows of the bushes and trees.

But the moonlight on the flats and along the slope of the hill calmed him, and it was with pleasure that he surveyed the night sky and felt the wind on his heavily bearded face. He was also glad not to be alone, to see the women trailing slowly behind him through the grass.

When he reached the top of the hill, where the grass was so thick he felt he was walking on an enormous haystack, he circled the grave several times, cursing its wooden shelter, which would hamper him when he raised his arm to pound the stake in. No matter where he stood, the roof was in the way, and he almost fell on his face trying to find a likely angle. At last he stuck the stake in the ground and walked around the grave one last time.

It was close to midnight, and the sties and huts and dugouts were sunk in darkness. The great autumn cold of grasses, water, and valleys spread out below him like an abyss, making the starry black sky seem near. He could see the women squatting in the underbrush, waiting for him to do the deed. Yet leaning against the log that held up the shelter, he shuddered and sweated in the night, alone, at the top of the hill, at the grave of the woman who had burst unexpectedly into his house. His house, for he considered Arandjel Isakovič's house his own.

Once she was put to rest, he thought, everyone could rest. Arandjel Isakovič would notice his daughter, and he, Ananije, would lead a peaceful existence in Vuk Isakovič's house until the man returned from the wars – if he did return. The entire village would live in peace. And after so many sleepless nights he would sleep again.

Pulling himself up to his full height, he gave the stake a blow with his mallet, but it merely fell over. He grabbed it, set it upright, and fell to pounding it like a madman. He was certain he heard it pierce first the earth, then the coffin, and finally the corpse.

The women, terrified by the sudden pounding, leaped up and raced down the hill, screaming and yelling, whereupon Ananije too took fright, bumped his head against the shelter, and missed the stake, which was deep in the ground by then.

The mallet came down hard on his leg. He fell flat across the grave, but managed to pick himself up, set off after the women, and, bellowing with pain and waking all the dogs and sheep, drag himself to the fence of his house. He even started climbing the fence, but the Evil One must have been waiting for him there, because his coat caught on a picket and he hung, eyes bulging, half strangled, until the dogs found him just before dawn and gnawed him free from the picket and the thorns, howling to his moans.

Nor had the women had an easy time of it. Lost in the shadows of night and fooled by the rays of the moon, they called back and forth to one another in vain and, tumbling into ditches, they covered their faces with their hands and skirts to keep from seeing the Evil One, who they knew was after them.

Stana fared the worst. She had joined Ananije's women less out of curiosity than out of fear of werewolves and vampires, which kept her awake and led her to ask so many questions about unearthly beings of her shepherd and swineherd lovers that they too grew afraid to go out at night. Running down the hill, she tripped near the first dugout and tumbled with a shriek into a large pit. Though up to her chest in the mud and weeds used by the peasants to build their hovels, she managed to hoist herself out, only to sink into a swamp, which would not let her go free, struggle as she might. Sobbing and screaming, frantic, exhausted, she nearly fainted at the sound of frogs all around her. Suddenly she saw the path to the village directly in front of her, yet completely out of reach. For all the times she had seen it by the light of day – it went straight past her hut – it looked eerie now and unfamiliar. She was so frightened, she could scarcely breathe. She felt the mud claiming her plump young body, filling its every curve, rising to her throat, ready to choke her. It reminded her of her wanton ways, her lovers, and finally her husband. She had heard that Vuk Isakovič had appeared to Dafina; would Arkadije now appear to her?

And then this small, round, usually scrubbed and cheerful young peasant girl with black curls, convinced she was dying, saw Arkadije sprawling in the mire before her, spread-eagled – as he had lain that evening near Stockstadt when two German peasants found him, took him by the arms and legs, and flung him into the Rhine – and she felt the absolute, unbridgeable gap between her, still alive and warm, and him, dead. But no, what Stana saw was only a figment of her frantic imagination, a play of swamp grass and moonlight in the swamp where she had sunk, screaming. Because Arkadije, the first casualty of the campaign, did not remain long in the Rhine or among the willows so similar to those of his country.

Vuk's orderly, still enveloped in the smell of his beloved horses, had been on the road for two months. Had risen from death and the water like a young acacia and traced his way back along the roads his regiment had travelled, back to where they once found him drunk and in a woman's skirts. Much as he stank of the sties in which he had grown to manhood, he was bound to life with so many fine white moonbeam threads that his wife had every right to sense his return to her on that autumn night. She merely sought him where he was not, and believed she had found him where he had not been.

Still lazy, so lazy he might have been sleepwalking, Arkadije did in fact enter the village that night, but from the other end, mumbling through his nose to a sow he had brought with him from Pécs. Radiant, transparent in the moonlight, he was so far removed from the events that had just taken place that his wife could not possibly have more than sensed his presence – a whiff from afar, a shade of the distant past. He appeared on the hill above the village and set off with his sow for his hut under the mulberry tree just as they were running away from Dafina's grave, frightened out of their wits.

No one could see him, and no one saw him. But the dogs moved out of his way.

When the sow came to a sudden halt at the entrance to the

village, the dead Arkadije tumbled over it, but he picked himself up, and, resuming his slow, somnambulant pace, moved on towards his hut, stopping only at a stable to inhale the smell of horses and revel in the sound of their stamping. Having arrived, white and transparent, at the door, he was not the least annoyed to find his wife's lovers, one of whom was sleeping half naked on the spot where his bed had once been; nor was he sad to hear the child cry. He did a little dance behind his sow.

Despite the screaming, the village remained sound asleep, and no one saw either Arkadije or the werewolves Ananije told the villagers about the next day.

As for Ananije, he was found half dead on the fence of Vuk Isakovič's house, mumbling something about having seen the dead Arkadije and heard him say he would not be coming home. By the time Stana was carried back to the hut, delirious from the horrors of the night, Arkadije was off inspecting Vuk's sties and patting the horses in the fields, as light and airy as smoke after a battle.

Several days later, when the village had calmed down from the strange events of that night, a man of flesh and blood, alive and perfectly visible, returned from the war. He was Sekula, the sexton – scalped, disfigured, one-eyed, and weeping. The stories he told roused the villagers to a frenzy, and they keened, old and young, from morning till night.

Ananije was the first to take pity on Sekula. To everyone's great surprise, he presented him with a sheep. "I stole it from you," he said, "and now, in the name of the Father and the Son and the Holy Spirit, I am giving it back to you." He added that it was wrong to steal and wrong to kill.

As the leg Ananije had struck with the mallet did not heal, he limped around the village while returning horses, sheep, and hay, all of which he had amassed during that spring and summer.

When word came that Vuk Isakovič and many of his men were alive and would be returning in the spring after spending the winter in Germany, the drums sounded and the whole village danced to fifes and pipes and drank mulberry *rakija*, crossing themselves and kissing one another, on the hill above the swamps and the turbulent Danube.

Shortly thereafter the blizzards began.

10

An Endless Blue Circle.
In It a Star

The winter of 1744 was long and hard. The Slavonian-Danubian Regiment, scattered among the towns and poverty-stricken hamlets of the Upper Palatinate, suffered greatly from the blizzards and biting cold. In stalls and stables and on hard, snow-encrusted earth under the bright icy sky, the men died of dysentery. They kept warm by keeping drunk, hopping up and down, and gathering around the fire, where to the strains of the gusla they lamented the fate of the legendary Prince Lazar. Then they would fall into a deep, unhealthy sleep, a sleep so heavy as to addle the wits. They slept and snored in barns and houses, attics and ditches, even dunghills, looting at night and returning at dawn, sad and weary.

Some of Vuk Isakovič's soldiers, enthralled by the beauty of the snow-swept woods and hills, went farther afield, roaming the countryside for days, until their strength gave out. Then they would drop in the snow and freeze. Others reached far-off villages and stayed away for weeks, mingling with the villagers. The guards would have to drag them back to camp, where they were whipped.

Accustomed to thinking and feeling as one man, the regiment now sensed that the great, terrible war that would bring it glory, uplift it, raise it to the very skies – this great war was not to be. As the wind swept away the traces of its wheels and hooves, so the silence of the German commanding officers on the subject of the regiment stilled all talk of battles and victories. The longer Vienna refrained from sending further instructions, the more the regiment felt like an unwanted guest in a foreign land.

Brown from sun and battle and pungent from gunpowder, its flags flying and its wounded dripping blood, the regiment initially appeared quite strange and terrifying to the local population. But after the first snows, this mass of ferocious alien beings was swallowed by silence and drifts and gradually fell out of sight. They made themselves felt, however, through their boundless virility, of which miracles were told in nearby villages. Released from drills, disbanded and hidden in dugouts, beneath haystacks and alongside fences, almost completely snowed in, the regiment would have gone unnoticed had it not been for the gusla and the wailing and keening that accompanied it, a din so terrible and piteous that it made the women weep.

Baron Bärenklau had disappeared, most of the Austrian officers had dispersed, and all that was left of the regiment was this band of tramps and ragamuffins. For a time sentries went on keeping guard here and there, by the carts in the snow; then they too disappeared.

The snow came up to the men's knees, then climbed tree trunks to bare branches. Flocks of crows cawed their way across the grey horizon. Packs of wolves appeared in the moonlight.

The regiment's blood-soaked glory was forgotten. The fact that so many men had perished seemed of no consequence. Everything had ended in misery. Everything froze, everything quivered in the fierce cold, and the days passed slowly.

Vuk Isakovič preferred living with the regiment to taking up quarters with the officers. Like a sick man, he lay all day, heavy as a log, wrapped in a sheepskin in his cart or stretched out on a bed of straw in the snow underneath it. As if deaf and dumb, he said not a word, standing only to stretch or transfer his sheepskin and blankets from the cart down to the wheels, from the wheels back up to the cart. He slept in fits and starts, in broad daylight, awakening and dozing off again at odd hours, tucking his head under the sheepskin. The only change in his existence came on the days he went fox-hunting, riding into the winter dawn or dusk with a profoundly miserable look on his face. He no longer made the rounds of his guards or even looked in on the men in their dugouts and huts. He scarcely responded to Bärenklau's orders and reports. His savage severity gone, he let the regiment go to seed, and for weeks failed even to inspect their weapons. His only concern was finding someone to take over for him while he slept.

His boots had lost all their colour from the mud and snow; they flopped down below his knees and made him look lop-sided and constantly intoxicated. His breeches, which drooped over his belly like a sack, were still red, but had long, pale streaks from water and sun; his belts and sashes sagged front and back. His silver-trimmed, fleece-lined greatcoats and tunics were so faded, threadbare, and tight that he had no hope of cutting a military figure and would stand listless by the cart, as if paralysed, arms hanging, head hanging. He had hanging jowls, hanging eyelids, hanging eyebrows and ears, and his hair, with no tricorn to hide it, hung down over his large flat nose. He not only failed to look the hero, he looked ready to meet his maker.

Leaning against a cartwheel, staring with swollen eyes at a long row of village houses and snow-covered trees, Vuk Isakovič felt none of the peace a bear feels in hibernation. Beneath the apparent lethargy of his physical being lurked acute despair: he felt constantly on the verge of jumping up, howling, dashing off madly, biting anything in his way, including himself, and everything inside him wept and quaked. His ribs were like knives chopping at his breath.

He had accepted the news of his wife's death with equanimity because it seemed to come from another world. Drained by his concern for the regiment, he lacked the strength even to shed a tear for her; he merely stood for a while by the boat in the murky water, stunned, then walked calmly back to camp. Neither at that time nor in the next few days did he show any disquiet in connection with his misfortune.

Inwardly, however, he felt that on that day his gallbladder or heart or intestines had burst. He fell prey to anxieties and remorse, to physical aches and spiritual distraction. That his sickly daughters were now motherless caused him no distress, but he did feel a certain compassion for his brother: Dafina's death must have been hard on him. The possibility that his brother had coveted his wife never entered his mind.

What tormented him most in the following days was that his wife's death had happened so abruptly, that it had no connection with him, her ceasing to exist, and that when he returned home – if he returned home – he would never see her again. The two of them had parted, gone separate ways, with no will to do so, no power to resist, no say in the matter. She was there, he here.

Just as his horses' hooves splashed the cart with mud, which he watched for days on end as he accompanied the regiment over the rough, snow-clogged roads, so the days, one by one, muddied the people and things he loved, his life, his soldiers, bringing them nothing but grief and woe, insults and horrors. The delay over his promotion to lieutenant colonel made his blood boil; the Austrians' frivolous approach to war – ordering one thing, then another, sending him here, then there – drove him insane. Sensing what awaited his people under the new emperor, he gazed upon his soldiers, horses, carts, and camps with terror, like a man awakening from a nightmare. In the deepest reaches of his memory, where he stored clouds and morning stars, he kept alive the trials of the regiment, the miserable roars of the men, their laments to the strains of the gusla, their terrifying charge into the fray, the death rattle of the dying, the howls of those forced to run the gauntlet, the faces of those hanged, the thrashing of Sekula, and the death of his dear Arkadije. Weary and mute, he heard their cries and their whispers, heard the whisper of the wheels, of the blankets stained with blood, of the sashes now tattered and the coats and boots removed from the fallen. But in the end there was only the void.

He gazed across the snowbound camps and villages to the woods, to the trees on the dark horizon. Where they were, where they had been – none of it seemed to exist any longer. All he could recall of the fighting on the Rhine was the boat that ran aground; of the battle at Severne, a single street. The arrest and court martial of Piščević, his best officer, had so galled him that his nose bled profusely and he gagged. But what shook him the most was the way the battle ended: they had fled, retreated into mud and snow, and were left to starve and shiver their way through the winter – with not one word of praise for the Serb regiments. He had been planted here like a scarecrow in the snow, with a greatcoat and nothing more – no money, no provisions – kept awake at night by crows, his horses freezing to death. And that was not all. He had heard talk at headquarters of their being sent home in the spring, a move every bit as senseless as the ones that had preceded it: more dead would be left in the earth, more broken-down carts by the wayside. Lieutenant Colonel Vuič told him they would be summoned to Vienna, but that turned out to be false. The days passed in unremitting fog and blizzards. The Slavonian-Danubian Regiment seemed consigned to oblivion. Isakovič's men had no idea what part of the world they were in.

The order to return home – a few scant words in German – arrived in early March. They were to follow approximately the same route they had taken before.

During the first weeks of spring the Slavonian-Danubian Regiment raced across Bavaria and Austria, whooping with joy and smashing tollgates as they went. They sang as they marched behind their officers; were impatient at halts, impossible at bivouacs. Even after the rains began, they gladly marched barefoot and into the night, but they were constrained by the official itinerary and so had to idle in various Styrian and Carniolan hamlets. They endured hunger and thirst without complaint, and did not miss the festive welcomes they had enjoyed on their way to battle.

Early in June, which was quite rainy that year, the first battalions of Vuič's regiments arrived home from the war with France. When the precise list of casualties became known, a great weeping and wailing arose in the villages up and down the Sava and the Danube.

Vuk Isakovič happened to be crossing the Drava at Osijek at the time, dragging what was left of his carts and boats in order to return them. He bivouacked near the Osijek ferry after a hard day's march with a large contingent of ill and wounded men. His regiment looked like a bank of invalids.

It was pouring. The men dispersed in the mud and tried to sleep. A mill creaked in the dark. The dripping willows, the puddles and swamps, the river quivering under the cloudburst – all told them they were close to home.

Vuk Isakovič stretched out beneath his cart on the ferry and covered himself with straw. He could not see the water, but he could smell it. He laid his head between the two wheels, their badly worn hubs dripping mud, and closed his eyes on this last night of the war. The next day he would be meeting Marquis Guadagni, who would review the troops and discharge them.

Petrovaradin and the village that had wailed at his departure and would wail at his return was still three days away, yet he could already hear the screaming and moaning and lamentations for the dead. Unable to sleep, he found himself contemplating, as he had so often in the recent past, what was best to do next. In three or four days, after he dismissed the troops and was alone again, he would be on the brink of madness, as surely as he was now on the banks of the Drava.

Several of his officers had spoken openly of returning to

Turkey, which their fathers had left, and many of the men were now talking of moving there with their families and sheep. Others spoke of Russia; General Stafan Vitkovič, one of the first to go there, whetted the appetites of many with his letters.

Battling with his soul on his last night as a soldier, Vuk Isakovič came to the conclusion that his life had been evil and that he needed to find a place where it could be good. Where he thought of his experiences with the Austrian army – on the ramparts, in the camps, on the battlefield – he saw how futile they had been. But when he thought of the swamps and the village he had shared with his brother and would have to visit again in a few days, he saw the same futility. Yet he brightened at the prospect of finishing his church in the centre of the village, and made up his mind that as soon as he arrived, he would commission an icon of Holy Prince Stefan Štiljanovič and leave it to the church after his death.

The end of hostilities, the winter in the Upper Palatinate, and the journey across Bavaria and Austria in the spring rains, painful as they had been, seemed a dream to him. Now that he was old, he had come to accept the idea of wandering lost, abstracted, and half asleep from one country to the next. Not until morning, when he awoke on the ferry and was faced with the task of readying the regiment for the review in Osijek, did reality – the turbid river, wet grass, trees, mills, bridge, town walls, ramparts, grey sky – strike him with full force. Once more he thought how vain the whole venture had been – fighting God knows where for God knows what reason. No one cared the slightest about the soldiers: they were driven like cattle to the slaughter; given flags to carry and plumes to wear and they were counted and recounted, dead or alive, like horses and cartridges; nor was there any connection between their wanderings from battlefield to battlefield and their home in the swamps. Moreover, Charles of Lorraine and Baron Bärenklau – indeed, the whole Austrian Empire – had simply been making a fool of him. The Governor had been abusive when they returned through Pécs, and the Marquis Guadagni would certainly badger him and laugh at the way the Slavonian-Danubian Regiment formed ranks or marched or did an about-turn.

He tried to drive away his black thoughts as he chased off his restless dogs, by leaping on his horse and thundering orders. The soldiers began running about, the drums began to roll, the officers flocked together. Within a few moments the Slavonian-Danubian Regiment had formed two long snake-like lines along the pontoon bridge – straight lines being still beyond its ability.

One last time! Vuk thought. One last chance to lead his men and show his mettle. On his horse he forgot the troubles and pain of his calling and thought of nothing but distinguishing himself. But galloping with his orderlies past the regiment, he so shook the bridge that he had to rein in his horse.

It was early. In the peaceful grey light of morning he could see the fortress, its casemate windows, its cannons, and the steep-roofed houses on the tree-lined bank. From the bridge the river looked wide, yellow, full of sand. The islands in the distance, the willows, the reeds were still and deep green. Instead of flinging his scabbard to an orderly according to custom, he drew his sabre slowly, clutching the hilt, and turned to the men.

An icy shiver ran down his back: it was the moment of infinite plenitude he so cherished.

But then, with the river flowing beneath his feet, the old squalid solitude returned, and, twisting his mustachio and pulling his tricorn down to his eyes, he gave his mount a spur and set off, trying hard to keep from bouncing like a barrel.

The soldiers set off after him, pounding the bridge like a cavalry unit. They too knew that this was their last review, and pressed onward, unkempt, unwashed, unshaven. Some were bareheaded, some lame; some were barefoot and enjoyed the feel of the swamp under their feet. They all sang at the top of their lungs. The officers, gathered around the flag, maintained a certain decorum, but the men seemed proud of their shredded coats and tattered trouser seats, their mud-caked boots, cracked rifles, and feet wrapped in rags.

Trudging through the wet sand along the bank, they entered the town gate and passed under a row of leafy acacias and along a wall with cannon barrels peeking out of the tall grass. Tramping through the mud, they could see the sky turn blue beyond the trees.

His sheepskin jerkin all plumes and silk ribbons again, Vuk Isakovič, bent low over his horse's neck, bounced along toward the main square. There, on a large balcony swarming with officers, Marquis Ascanio Guadagni stood waiting to be shown the remains of the regiment, a list of the dead, and the proper honour and respect.

The last time! thought Vuk. He had had enough of skirmishing his way across Italy, of stalking the Rhine and prowling the Danube. It was high time he realized they would never make him a lieutenant colonel. Things would be better in Russia. True, he was not born to be a merchant, but even a merchant's life would be better than the pointless, bestial life he had been living. Had he been anything but a soldier, he would have settled down peacefully with his wife and daughters, and his wife might still be alive.

Yet was there anything so fine as the life of a soldier? Why the constant desire to settle down on the part of his brother, whom he would meet in Petrovaradin in three days? What awaited him there? Two children he had no idea what to do with. A village he wished to expand up the hillside, before moving to Russia, where he still intended to live. Swamps, winter drills in Petrovaradin, the dreaded summons to Vienna, and the illness of the Patriarch, of which he had learned only recently and which disturbed him greatly.

Lulled by the echo of the hooves, he was surprised to find

himself in the square, and started when he saw a long row of cannons chained together and a crowd of officers and artillerymen. From the balcony, which jutted out from headquarters' enormous windows and was decorated profusely with flags, plumes, ribbons, breastplates, and cocked hats, a fuming General Guadagni was signalling Isakovič to start the procession immediately.

Caught off guard but trained to obey his commanding officer, he immediately cleared his mind of his troubles, pulled up his mount so brutally that the animal reared and danced about on its hind legs, and shouted, "Charge!" Closing his eyes and ears to everything in his desire to correct the General's first impression, forgetting the perfectly reasonable instructions he had been given the night before, he lost his head like an old woman and shouted new commands left and right, running the troops up and down, back and forth, in two ranks and in six, rifles down and in the air, daggers drawn and pistols in hand, kneeling, jumping, sprawling on the ground. And through it all he rode up and down the ranks, brandishing his sabre and spurring on his horse, rearing it beneath the General's balcony and shouting "*Vivat* Marquis Guadagni! *Vivat* Marquis Guadagni!" while the bedecked and bedizened General Guadagni wrung his hands in despair over the wild Serb's antics, and so close to the balcony.

But why go on about how the Slavonian-Danubian Regiment disgraced itself that day? Besides, considering that the officers eventually did bring the troops under control – though not until after they had tried to storm the cannons – and behaved in exemplary military fashion, one might say that it all ended well. Even General Guadagni revised his attitude when he heard how many of the regiment's men had fallen in battle.

But Vuk Isakovič would not have cared had they clapped him in irons. When called to the balcony, he did not waste time apologizing; at the noon meal in the ceremonial hall he got roaring drunk with the cuirassiers; and in the evening he fell asleep in the General's private salon.

All through the day he trembled at the thought of how close he was to home, to the house in which he had lived with his wife. He was angry at the idea of returning alive to a place he had believed he would never see again. Every bend in the river, every inch of the hillside ran through his mind; every care, every woe. He saw flashes of faces, some dear, others loathsome, and the closer he came to home, the greater concern he felt for dear sweet Orthodoxy and for his wife's grave. He had so hoped to avoid the weeping and wailing; he had so hoped to avoid the return.

He left Guadagni's house at midnight after the farewell banquet, with a rumbling stomach and the sadness that as usual accompanied it. The wet night, the empty square, and the shadows cast by the ramparts so unnerved him that he nearly slipped down some steps. Captain Antonovič, who happened to leave shortly after, helped him the rest of the way. In an attempt to make conversation, Antonovič brought up the portrait of Isakovič the General planned to have commissioned for Vienna at the army's expense in recognition of his part in the Bärenklau campaign. But Isakovič looked him calmly in the eye and said that only saints were immortal and he would not allow his image to be graven. He would, however, commission an image of Holy Prince Stefan Štiljanovič at his own expense to remain here below when he, Vuk Isakovič, was gone.

Indeed, he felt so old and ailing the next morning as he rode out of Osijek, that he hardly cared whether he lived or died.

The crowd that gathered at the bridge to watch the troops depart, however, saw only a dignified warrior and felt nothing but respect for his age and deeds.

Listening to the cadence of his men's feet as they marched along with quartered sheep on their backs and sang about the taking of Belgrade, hearing the ring of his officers' laughter as they sat cross-legged in their saddles, Turkish-style, waving their sabres, puffing on their pipes, and calling out to the young women – Isakovič pranced out in front, stately, well-groomed, medals shining, bright eyes gazing into the distance, with a vague smile masking his despair.

For the last time in his life he was handsome.

By the time he had ridden past the fortress, through the huge arch of the town gate, and on to the bridge over the river with its view of green willows and blue sky, the hand that held the sabre hung low, its strength gone. He had done what needed to be done, but the fatigue from all the dreadful nights he had been through and from the long march and the review now fell squarely on him. The moist scent of the trees, the sultry heat of the low sun-baked clouds, and the mist rising like smoke from the water had a stifling, soporific effect on him, and he became calm – as when he had set out many months before, putting misfortune behind him and having a clear distance ahead. He expected to reach Petrovaradin on the third day, before dark. Then, after dismissing several units, he would follow orders and report to Baron Engelshofen, commanding officer at Temesvár.

Like his father, whose name he invoked whenever he had something important to say, he returned from the war with a mute sadness, a stubborn, old man's silence. He was tired of migrating, tired of the restlessness that plagued the people he led as much as it plagued him. If he left the army, he would have to join his brother and travel as a tradesman from town to town, his daughters in tow; if he remained in the army, he would still be forced to travel, his duty being to pacify the migrating populations.

He knew he could expect nothing but grief at home, yet he viewed the years, events, and people ahead of him with confidence and equanimity.

Heavy with sleep, he rode across the bridge towards the tall grass with his head bent. The warmer and lighter the day became, the heavier he felt, and the sway of the horse sapped his remaining strength. What he had left behind seemed never to have been, while his wife's death and the coming meeting with his brother and the tears of his two girls had merged with the mist. His orderlies, officers, and men having dropped behind, he felt utterly alone. Riding along the sandy bank and mulling over how to persuade the General to accept the officers' requests for transfer to other regiments, he dozed off. All one need do, he thought, is move away, and everything one leaves behind will be as nought.

He opened his eyes to a range of hills and a burst of silver that was the sun emerging from them. He felt tired and empty and so light as to have no body; then he felt warm from the sun and as transparent as the wind at his back. He broke into a trot.

Once more, before facing Arandjel and all his troubles, he began to think about Russia. He was still resolved to settle there with his children and his men; it was the only escape from the wretched, sorry, miserable future awaiting him if he stayed at home. Why should it be impossible to go off and lead a carefree existence, take the men with him, give them a happy, easy life? There had to be a bright place somewhere; one had only to find it.

Russia was a fairy-tale kingdom. He had heard of people flocking there from all over the world, making their fortunes and rising immediately in rank. Life there, domestic and military, was noble, the churches beautiful, the Orthodoxy sweet. While all that awaited him here was poverty, the endless grief that had robbed him of his sanity, and a void that had spread out before him and his old age.

The only image he could summon up of the past was one of pure silver stars and of woodland paths with April mists descending on them from the hills he was now approaching, the hills where he had lived in the early days of his union with the wife to whose grave and children he was now returning.

A void before him, the past irrevocably gone. He had gained

nothing from this war, nothing from the previous ones, and his wanderings had continued unabated. Deep in his heart, however, he felt certain that things could not go on as they had; a voice promised him something extraordinary at the end.

In the void, in the bottomless pit before him, he saw his life, his children, the death of his wife, the lot of his brother, the return of his men, the weeping and wailing of the womenfolk; he saw that his life was over and he could not set it right, nor could he set right the lives of the men who had followed him and were now returning to the marshes. Yet he did not feel he was born for the unspeakable boredom and emptiness that he saw around him and that had led him to similar thoughts during his lethargy in the hut outside Strasbourg.

There had to be a better life somewhere, a life like cool, fresh waters coming together in foaming cascades. That was why he needed to migrate. He would find the proper place, a place as pure, limpid, and smooth as the surface of a deep mountain lake, a place where he could live a peaceful existence, live as he pleased, far from this awful chaos, live the life he was born to live, a glorious life that hovered above him as surely as the sky did.

It was raining when he arrived at Petrovaradin, raining on the ramparts, on the river, the bridge, the trees. The troops were soaked and spattered with mud. Women and old men came up to them with bread, *rakija*, and clean clothes, weeping and wailing for the dead. The soldiers sang, drank, threw straw, and embraced one another. Soon enough the whole town had heard that the Slavonian-Danubian Regiment, along with the other Serb regiments, would be disbanded and its members distributed among random imperial regiments like ordinary peasants or servants, and that all those who objected would have to pack their belongings and go elsewhere.

Having expected his brother to come and greet him, Vuk pivoted angrily on his horse when he heard that Arandjel had sent his servants instead, and that they were waiting for him on the outskirts of town in a large boat. Not until evening, exhausted from the women's keening and the tallying of men and firearms, could he make his way down to the spot on the river near the bridge, which reminded him of the river in Austria where he had learned of his wife's death. There he found his orderlies standing around a man wrapped in several wet coats and lying on a wet trunk that jutted from the water. Darkness was falling, rain streaming down, but the man recognized Vuk and limped over to him. It was Ananije, Arandjel's old servant.

Arandjel was not there to welcome him, he said, because he had moved into a new house in Buda; they would have ample time to see each other later.

Vuk's daughters were in good health and living in Vuk's house; Arandjel had provided well for them.

Arandjel had had a shelter built for Dafina's grave.

The church was under construction.

Vuk's orderly, Arkadije, had been haunting the village at night, singing through his nose and frightening his own wife.

The cattle had been visited by a pestilence.

And the wall on the hill side of his house had cracked badly and was about to cave in.

After paying his respects to Dafina's grave the next evening, Vuk approached his house for the first time. The women so wept and wailed for their dead that he was forced to take refuge inside.

Everything was as he had left it – the willows rising in the mist, the clouds tumbling, the land black, invisible, rain-soaked. Intermittent barking came to him, the same as ever, and the dull thud of hooves nearby, as if from underground.

Lying on his back with his eyes wide open but so tired that he could scarcely speak, Vuk looked on bewildered while Ananije and his wife and daughters bustled about in the semidarkness with straw and buckets of hot water. After the others had left, the youngest girl kept fussing, leaning over him with her ample breasts and broad hips.

Before he could even undress, he sank into a deep torpor. He had been drinking since early morning. Only now did he truly feel that he had come home, home to the swamps, to the river that filled the night with its murmur, to the floods and bogholes and gullies, to the endless luxuriant willows.

Later he ordered his bed made up, and Ananije and his family ran for quilts, sheepskins, and silk sheets. Again the ample-breasted, broad-hipped daughter stayed the longest. Vuk observed the white flesh of her legs by the weak light and, old, weary, and moribund as he was, felt his body come alive and swell. Surprised, he went over to the door half naked and tugged it open. He heard the scrape of the well sweep.

It was night. Rain fell noiselessly over the meadow, through the trees, into the sties, down the fields. Again he felt the all-encompassing damp of the marshes and reeds. After several loud sneezes and a stamp of the foot so powerful that everything around him shook, he turned back to the dark of the room and the warmth of the hearth and dropped with all his weight on to the bed.

When the girl came up to him once more – leaning over him, seeming to circle the bed with her large round breasts and thighs – he gave a hollow cough and, his heart in his mouth, told her to go. Like rain finding its way to a seed in the depths of the earth, the blood in his brain flowed to a single glittering point, the last firm outpost of purity of thought. Ill at ease, he bent his head as if to inspect his sabre, the tassels on his tricorn, the pistols under his pillow, but in fact it was to keep his eyes from her bounteous body. He told himself that he had to rise early the next morning to go and see the Patriarch, and make ready for his journey to Vienna, and save his men from new migrations and the confiscation of their arms, and decide what to do about his daughters, and visit his brother in Buda and Baron Engelshofen in Temesvár, and buy new carts and horses, and build a smithy for the village, and arrange for Captain Antonovič's transfer, and write a detailed report on the return of the Slavonian-Danubian Regiment, and most important, most important of all, devise a plan whereby he could go to Russia, where he had long since hoped to live.

Outside, the rain was still falling, the women – near the sties, under the mulberry trees – still weeping and wailing over their dead.

Thus, in 1745, in early summer, did Vuk Isakovič come home from the wars.

And, haunted by thoughts revolving in an infinite circle, thoughts of leaving, leaving for Russia, the only relief from the despair and tedium of months of wandering and suffering, he fell asleep again in his own bed, his body trembling like a star, the final seed of his former youth, a seed that sustained him – silent, despondent, all but demented with misery and grief among the marshlands and waters that rose up over the land he lovingly called New Serbia – a seed that even in his old age retained the power to grow and burgeon and bring forth new beings beyond time and the heavens, who would be reflected, as arching bridges were reflected, in the waters that flowed and met here between Turkey and Austria.